A Concise History of the
Sex Manual 1886–1986

A Concise History
of the
Sex Manual
1886-1986
by Alan Rusbridger
illustrated
by Posy Simmonds

ff

faber and faber

LONDON · BOSTON

First published in 1986 by
Faber and Faber Limited
3 Queen Square London WC1N 3AU
Filmset by Wilmaset
Birkenhead Wirral
Printed in Great Britain by
Redwood Burn Limited
Trowbridge Wiltshire
All rights reserved

British Library Cataloguing in Publication Data

Rusbridger, Alan
A concise history of the sex manual 1886–1986
1. Sexual intercourse
I. Title   II. Simmonds, Posy
613.9′6   HQ31
ISBN 0–571–13519–6
ISBN 0–571–14547–7 (Pbk)

Contents

Acknowledgements

Helen Gurley Brown, *Having it All*, 1982, Sidgwick and Jackson (London) and Simon and Schuster (New York). By permission of Irving Lazaar.

Paul Brown and Carolyn Faulder, *Treat Yourself to Sex: A Guide for Good Loving*, 1977, J. M. Dent and Sons Limited. By permission of David Higham Associates Limited.

Philip Cauthery and Drs Andrew and Penny Stanway, *The Complete Book of Love and Sex: A Guide for All the Family*, 1983, Century Hutchinson (London) and Stein and Day (New York). By permission of Rupert Crew Limited.

Barry Chant, *Straight Talk About Sex*, 1977, used by permission of the publisher, Whitaker House, Pitsburg and Celfax Streets, Springdale, Pennsylvania 15144, USA.

Dr Eustace Chesser, *Love Without Fear: A Plain Guide to Sex Technique for Every Married Adult*, 1941, Rich and Cowan. Reprinted by permission of Century Hutchinson.

Dr Eustace Chesser, *Woman and Love*, 1962, Jarrolds. Reprinted by permission of Century Hutchinson and International Literary Management.

Alex Comfort, *The Joy of Sex*, 1972, Quartet Books (London) and Crown Publishers (New York).

Alex Comfort, *More Joy of Sex*, 1975, Mitchell Beazley (London) and Simon and Schuster (New York).

Jane Cousins, *Make It Happy: What Sex is All About*, 1978, Virago Press Limited (London) and Viking Penguin Inc. (New York).

Dr M. J. Exner, *The Sexual Side of Marriage*, 1932, George Allen and Unwin (London) and W. W. Norton and Company Inc. (USA).

Nancy Friday, *My Secret Garden*, 1983, Quartet Books (London) and Pocket Books (New York).

Norval Geldenhuys, *The Intimate Life, Or the Christian's Sex Life: A Practical Up-to-date Handbook Intended for Engaged and Newly-Married Christians*, 1952, James Clarke and Company Limited (Cambridge).

Harvey Gochros and Joel Fischer, *Treat Yourself to a Better Sex Life*, 1980, Prentice-Hall, Inc., Englewood Cliffs, New Jersey, USA.

Eleanor Hamilton, *Sex Before Marriage*, 1971, George Allen and Unwin Limited. Reprinted by permissions of Lawrence Pollinger Limited and the Meredith Corporation.

9

ACKNOWLEDGEMENTS

Anthony Havil, *Toward a Better Understanding of Sexual Relationships*, 1939, Wales Publishing Company.

Julia Heiman, Leslie Lopiccolo and Joseph Lopiccolo, *Becoming Orgasmic: a Sexual Growth Program for Women*, 1976, Prentice-Hall Inc., Englewood Cliffs, New Jersey, USA.

Isabel Emslie Hutton, CBE, MD, *The Hygiene of Marriage*, 1953, Heinemann (London).

'J', *The Sensuous Woman: The First How-to Book for the Female who Yearns to be an All Woman*, 1970, Lyle Stuart Inc., New Jersey, USA.

Sheila Kitzinger, *Woman's Experience of Sex*, 1983, Dorling Kindersley (London) and Putnam Publishing Group Inc. (New York).

Tim and Beverly LaHaye, *The Act of Marriage*, 1976, Zondervan Corporation, used by permission.

Marabel Morgan, *The Total Woman*, 1973, Hodder and Stoughton (London) and Fleming H. Revell Company (New Jersey). Used by permission of Fleming H. Revell Company.

National Sex Forum, *SAR (Sexual Attitude Restructuring) Guide for a Better Sex Life*, 1975.

Joseph Nowindski, *Becoming Satisfied: A Man's Guide to Self-Fulfilment*, 1980, Prentice-Hall, Inc., Englewood Cliffs, New Jersey, USA.

Gilbert Oakley, *Sane and Sensual Sex*, 1963, Walton Press (London).

Alexandra Penney, *How to Make Love to a Man*, 1981, Clarkson N. Potter Inc. (New York).

Wardell B. Pomeroy, *Girls and Sex*, 1969, Delacorte Press.

Lucia Radl, MD, *Illustrated Guide to Sex Happiness in Marriage*, 1953, Heinemann.

William S. Sadler, *Courtship and Love*, 1952, Macmillan Publishing Company (New York). Copyright renewed 1980. Used by permission of Macmillan Publishing Company.

George Ryley Scott, *Your Sex Questions Answered*, 1947, Knowle Park Press (Sevenoaks).

Lewis Smedes, *Sex in the Real World*, 1976, William B. Eerdmans Publishing Company (Grand Rapids).

Marilyn A. Tithram and William E. Hartman, *Any Man Can*, 1985, J. Aronson.

L. D. Weatherhead, *The Mastery of Sex Through Psychology and Religion*, 1932, Macmillan Publishing Company (New York). Renewed 1959 by L. D. Weatherhead. Reprinted with permission of the publisher.

Helena Wright, MB, BS, *Sex, An Outline for Young People*, 1963, Ernest Benn Limited.

Introduction

No, of course you have never read one. Do not think me disrespectful
if I say no one ever has. You will, of course, have thumbed through
the copy of *The Joy of Sex* that Peter and Alison keep in their spare
room and you naturally have vague recollections of a worthy work of
pubescent instruction given you by your parents that dwelled at
superfluous lengths upon the rabbit. But, no, you have never
actually *read* one to speak of. Let alone bought one.

It is, let us be fair, a hard thing to own up to in polite company.
Why were you reading it? – Out of need? But of course not.
Curiosity? No, no. Just a bit of fun, really. Learn much? Oh, really.
And yet millions of the things have been sold to someone. Millions
of copies; thousands of books, and not all of them for a bit of fun.

The first sex manual I came across was a battered paperback
passed around at school. It was, as I remember, called *The
Marriage Art* and was considered to be pretty fruity. Particularly
striking to the adolescent mind was advice on the benefits to a
marriage that would accrue from the art of dexterous and timely
use of a polythene bag full of crushed ice. Unhappily, our studies
were curtailed when *The Marriage Art* was confiscated by a master
who, for all I know, may still own it.

Around the same time I came across a work of greater
scholarship on the subject of adolescence by one Prof. G. Stanley
Hall and was fascinated to find huge tracts devoted to the question
of masturbation. The discovery was made in the late 1960s, the
uneasy no man's land in the history of onanism between the time
when it made you go mad and the time when you were mad not to.
But nothing I had heard about Victorian treatises on the subject
lived up to the alarmingness of Prof. Hall's admonishments.
Insanity and blindness were of the least concern to those tempted
to play with themselves. How were they going to explain away the
purple, clammy skin, the dwarfing, the dry cough, the baldness,
the stoop, the anorexia and the 'digestive perversions'?

But the school library also boasted a grubbily thumbed copy of Kinsey's 1949 volume on *Sexual Behaviour in the Human Male*, which proved conclusively that 92.1 per cent of the male American population had masturbated by the age of twenty at an average rate of 2.4 times a week. Self-evidently, nowhere near 92.1 per cent of the American population was composed of purple-skinned, stooping, bald, anorexic dwarfs. Prof. G. Stanley Hall, I concluded, told whoppers.

It was but a short step from there to the discovery that whoppers were not limited to the solitary forms of sex, and that an enormous number had been published about the more companionable varieties. Again, one knew about the Victorians – or thought one did – but was less *au fait* with the range and daring of the whoppers that poured out during the twentieth century, and still do. Pity the pregnant woman in the 1920s told by rival authors both that sex might cripple her unborn child – or that abstaining from sex might do the same. And pity a teenager in the 1980s torn between advice that pre-marital sex is just fine and the warnings of an evangelist Christian writer that it could lead to a mental institution.

The Concise History of the Sex Manual over the past hundred or so years is not concerned with the big names in sexology – Ellis, Freud, Kinsey, Masters and Johnson. It is about the outpourings of an odd assortment of clerics, doctors, scoutmasters, sociologists, schoolmasters, feminists, opportunists and plain dirty old men. Some are well-intentioned, some bigoted, some ignorant, some enlightened, some funny, some dull, some dishonest. Some are household names; others are barely known. Most of them enjoyed – and still enjoy – huge sales and an extraordinary influence.

Researching the subject has not been easy. A peculiar form of nerve is required to walk into a bookshop in Camden Town and purchase £82.50 worth of sex manuals. A particular dedication is called for when asking at the London Library for a book considered so smutty that it is kept not on the open stacks but in the Chief Librarian's own office. The eventual selection of manuals is more or less random and by and large represents the first eighty or so that I came across. Another book, just as representative, could doubtless be written on the basis of a different eighty. There is no shortage of manuals to choose from.

A number of friends, colleagues and relatives have been good enough to help out with suggestions, advice and the odd review copy. They are unanimous in the view that the kindest acknowledgement of their help would be for them to remain quite incognito. Thanks, all the same.

First

Nights

We should begin on honeymoon, for that is where so many writers on such matters would approve of us beginning. And here to guide us through this delicate and bewitching period, we have Dr Gilbert Oakley, D.Psy., author of *Sane and Sensual Sex*. We are already in the bridal suite and Dr Oakley wishes to emphasize that our husband should regard his new bride 'as a highly sensitized human being'. He tells the husband that his wife might wish him to undress her. 'This act of subjugation', he advises him reassuringly, 'is very often encountered and the psychology of it is the primitive urge for masculine possession coupled with the fancied scene of the man taking the girl by storm and stripping her against her will.' Nothing to worry about.

With Dr Oakley's couple the wife does indeed wish to be undressed. Our husband is a little unsure of his ground here, so Dr Oakley obliges further. 'The husband should not hesitate to undress his newly-wed wife with delicacy, with obvious admiration for her underwear and finally, for her body itself. He should not seem to be too gloating, but should reduce her, with his eyes, his touch and with the things he may say to her, to the imagined status of a small girl who is helpless and resigned at his hands.' For that is where Dr Oakley wants her, *vis-à-vis* his husband. The doctor's bride 'has spent considerable time and thought over her trousseau, as well as cash'. And so? 'So the husband should duly observe each article of clothing as he strips her, with appreciation and pleasure. Her underwear, especially, must make an impression on him, for it is these intimate garments upon which she will have lavished most care. Indeed, he will be wise to ask her to parade around a while in her bra and panties before these, too, are taken from her. A female is most conscious of these two garments – final borderline between respectability and complete nudity.' Is nudity not respectable? But come now; the husband, too, must be getting undressed. It is, says, Dr Oakley, a delicate matter, even though 'most women are used to seeing men in bathing trunks and slips on the beaches'.

There are niceties in male underwear, too, and the wise bridegroom 'will not reveal himself to his wife in clumsy-looking, long-legged pants with buttons down the front, neither will he wear extravagantly big "boxer shorts" that he feels look manly but which, to her, will probably look funny. He will choose to wear continental-style briefs, high-cut and smart in white or a pastel shade.' Oh, and he can throw away that flappy singlet too. When his bride first lifts his eyes he will be completely nude – except for the pastel briefs.

More and more delicate are the steps now to be trodden, for sooner rather than later the husband must remove those smart pastel briefs and his wife must see what has previously remained engirdled in bathing trunks on beaches – 'a sight of terror for her or, at most unwelcome'. The wise husband has this in mind and 'will try so to control himself that his genitals are in a normal state at first sight so that his wife will not immediately get the impression of over-eagerness, lust or overpowering masculine aggressiveness'.

But it should not be thought that Dr Oakley has no words for his bride. He tells her of her instinctive urge to be dominated and of man's inherent desire that she should admire his phallus. Indeed, he is quite severe in this matter. 'It is lax and unwise of a girl to ignore, through moral prudery, squeamishness or misplaced moral upbringing, this part of a man's body, only accepting it as a means of giving her body pleasure . . . A female has little to no argument in revolting against the sight of male testicles and penis. It may well be that in them she sees a potential "weapon" of aggression but since woman's ultimate goal *is* to be attacked (in the nicest possible way) by *just* this weapon, denial of its existence appears merely hypocritical. This is also a selfish view as she is only too ready to take it into her body for the pleasure of it and to make sure she becomes a mother. To discard it and only to use it for this purpose is immature.'

The inquisitive may by now be wondering about Dr Oakley himself, his passionate concern for underwear and his Janet and John conception of the female psyche. The preface is of some help here in telling us that *Sane and Sensual Sex* is 'the result of a lifetime of research into the sexual imbalances of man and woman'. That this isn't entirely true we can deduce from the dust-jacket, which indicates that Dr Oakley's lifetime has been crowded with a glut of other research subjects. They reel off like chapter headings from *Readers' Digest*: 'Success Through Self-analysis', 'Better Health from Health Foods and Herbs', 'How to Cultivate Confidence and Promote Personality', 'Making Friends – the Key to Success', 'Project Telstar', 'Successful Salesman to Sales-Manager', 'Public Speaking', 'Self-Hypnosis' and 'How to Read Character Through Handwriting'. Add 'Humour in Uniform' and you more or less have a ready-made omnibus edition. But the most startling fact about *Sane and Sensual Sex* is its date, which is not 1923, nor even 1943, but 1963. The Lady Chatterley case had come and gone, as Dr Oakley points out in his introductory remarks. 'The public are now used to frequently seeing two people in the same bed together on the screen and on TV – the relationship of man and woman in the intimacy of the sexual plane is far more freely exploited.' And here in 1963 is Dr Oakley, eager and willing to exploit it more freely still. 'This book is the most up-to-date treatise on the oldest subject in the world,' he enthuses. 'It takes the "X" out of Sex.' And, what's more, it's illustrated.

Fortunately we have other authorities than Dr Oakley to guide us through those first anxious days and weeks following the wedding. Not only anxious, but crucial. 'Marriages', Dr Eustace Chesser tells readers of *Love without Fear* in 1941, 'can largely be made or marred on the honeymoon.' Presumably marred in the case of the lady quoted by Dr M. J. Exner in 1932: 'I felt raped and hated him from that moment on.' Two hundred and thirty-seven out of 925 women interviewed in a study cited by Dr Exner felt repelled by their husbands during their first sexual encounters in marriage; a further 223 felt neutral. Many manual-writers advise delaying intercourse after the marriage for days or even weeks. Some even suggest postponing the honeymoon itself. Dr L. B. Sperry (*Confidential Talks with Husband and Wife*, 1900) recommends staying at home for a few months before taking a 'wedding journey', adding: 'It is the time for the husband to show himself A MAN, instead of a selfish sensualist or a careless and ungovernable brute.'

Subsequent writers agree. Moreover, they share Dr Oakley's concerns about the visual impact of that which it was to be sincerely hoped brides had hitherto no cause to encounter – save,

naturally, in bathing trunks. Most writers stop short of Dr
Oakley's drooling over 'several inches of living, hard flesh', but Dr
Theodore van de Velde warns in 1926 that 'to display the male
member, which would seem gigantic to her unaccustomed eyes,
would only terrify her and accentuate her unconscious psychic
dread' while Dr Chesser thinks any virgin would consider the penis
'HUGE'. 'Instances could be cited', he adds in support, 'of brides
who have fled from the bedroom when, on their wedding night, the
husbands, eager to impress them with their sexual endowment,
have displayed themselves.' 'Gigantic proportions', bubbles E.
Parkinson-Smith in 1952. Dr Isabel Emslie Hutton is only slightly
less impressed the following year: 'fairly large and not particularly
aesthetic . . . don't be shocked . . . and don't jump to the
conclusion that there is not room enough.'

Accordingly, the husband should take things easy – and there is
no doubt in most writers' minds that it is the husband who must
call the shots, even where it is conceded (which is not very often)
that the bride might have some previous form. Chesser strongly
advises against waiting for the wife to request intercourse. 'That
would be relinquishing the man's role as initiator and educator . . .
The normal woman likes to feel herself conquered. The masterly
touch of her lover is invariably pleasing.' Normal women, says
Chesser, expect their husbands to 'take them', and 'extreme
nervousness on the man's part, undue hesitation – anything which
robs the act of spontaneity, will immediately lower her estimate of
her lover.' 'The husband', says Parkinson-Smith, 'is usually the
initiator.' 'The burden of education', says Isabel Hutton in 1953,
'is squarely on your broad masculine shoulders.'

And what a dead weight it is for chaps. For, while never
flinching or swerving from their task, they must come to terms with
the fact that (a) all their wife's instincts until this moment were to
regard what they are about to embark upon as the work of the
Devil; and (b) that one false move and psychic dread may set in for
life. Listen to what the seers say! Chesser's forties' brides will
instinctively recoil from 'full congress' since it means 'losing
something which has been carefully protected'. Something?
Parkinson-Smith is less guarded, speaking of 'the wife's virginal
modesty – a treasure in itself', while William Sadler in *Courtship
and Love*, 1952, reminds the husband that 'his wife has been
brought up to resist the sexual advances of all men and to defend

her chastity with her life'. Hence the feeling 'almost of repulsion' which Isabel Hutton's fifties' brides can be expected to feel at 'the something rather unpleasant which they will have to put up with'.

Is there no advice for bridegrooms understandably daunted by the task facing them? Indeed there is. Practically-minded Parkinson-Smith advises approaching the matter by lamplight or fireglow, 'if only to avoid clumsiness'. Chesser advises husbands to delay weeks, if necessary, before 'seducing your wife by all means'. Hutton thinks it better to get it over with straight away, so as to avoid strain building up, but is blunt with her husbands: 'Don't rape your bride.' The Reverend Barrington O. Burrell in *Love, Sex and Marriage*, 1983, is another one in favour of direct action, but for more mundane reasons. 'A sexual release would help them to relax and have a good night's sleep.'

But please don't run away with the idea that it's going to be enjoyable. 'There is not much likelihood of specific gratification for her in the first sexual act, which makes her a woman,' warns van de Velde. 'Don't expect much', says Isabel Hutton, 'and you won't be disappointed. You [and here she addresses her brides] probably will not experience the much-discussed "orgasm" during the first intercourse. But don't be disappointed. You have several decades of married life ahead of you.' There's a comfort. So, moderation please from both of you. Your honeymoon 'should not be a riot of love', says ever-sober van de Velde, who sees the post-wedding period as the first days at 'married life school . . . an apprenticeship for her.' Not that the husband hasn't lessons to grapple with, too. Tim and Beverly LaHaye's husband in *The Act of Marriage*, 1976, is learning to give his wife orgasms – but not, naturally, a riot of them: 'twice will probably be sufficient at this stage of the marriage'. Tim and Beverly's wife is also entering an apprenticeship. 'Before beginning this exercise, the wife should have several tissues on hand.' Homely, Tim and Beverly.

The LaHayes and their fellow religious writers apart, honeymoon homilies begin to fade from the manuals around the mid-sixties, when husbands could no longer assume as Isabel Hutton could in the early fifties, that 'the chances are that you will be better informed on sexual matters than she will'. Advice on defloration becomes less urgent in tone, though one wonders how urgently-needed it ever was. Alex Comfort, in *The Joy of Sex* (1972), considers it peculiar that such an obsession should have stopped being a problem – he puts it down to the fashion for petting and a shift in sexual attitudes. In fact seventy-two years earlier, the American Dr Sperry is already noting slightly sourly that the hymen is 'absent quite as frequently as it is perceptibly present; indeed, in this country it seems almost to have gone out of fashion'. Sad, sad – especially when, according to Comfort, it is such a fruitful and nostalgic source of fantasy. Why not celebrate an anniversary in this way, he suggests: '. . . deflower her again "playwise", honeymoon hotel and all. All she needs to do is to say "Tonight, I'm a virgin." ' But not quite all, surely? There is the trousseau, the underwear, the smart pastel continental-style briefs . . . but such Jabberwocky outings must wait awhile.

2

Animal Passions: Human Skills

Who needs sex manuals, anyway? The most obvious answer is that authors and publishers do since there are few subjects that can match sex for sheer shelf-stamina, sales figures and profits. None, in fact, bar the Bible and the odd dictionary. Look no further than the example of the afore-mentioned Theodore van de Velde, the Dutch gynaecologist and author of over eighty books and papers who, at the age of fifty-three, brought out his explicit and copiously illustrated magnum opus, *Ideal Marriage*, amidst mournful predictions of its consequences for himself. 'It will have many unpleasant results for me,' he laments in his personal introductory statement. 'I know this, for I have gradually attained to some knowledge of my fellow human beings and of their habit of condemning what is unusual and unconventional.' He writes through duty alone and out of the knowledge that he 'could not face the evening of my life with a quiet conscience if I omitted to do so'.

So condemnatory was the reading public that the German edition alone went through forty-two printings in eight years before being suppressed when Hitler came to power. The English translation, published by Heinemann in 1930, went through more than forty printings and sold more than a million copies, while the American Random House edition has sold more than half a million since 1945. The American sales pre-1945, Pan Books edition in Britain and the numerous other translations around the world all helped to ensure that the results for van de Velde himself were far from unpleasant, and he ended his days in some comfort living in Switzerland with his second wife – a former patient he had eloped with in 1909. His book was still in print thirty years after his death in 1937 and was still cited as an authority until the mid-sixties.

The only person to manage comparable figures since van de Velde is, of course, Alex Comfort, whose Quartet edition of *The Joy of Sex* has sold between 80,000 and 100,000 every year since its publication in 1972 – and that is simply counting the UK and Commonwealth rights. The sequel, *More Joy of Sex*, has averaged between 50,000 and 65,000 a year. Not that there haven't been some pretty impressive rivals to these two. Tim and Beverly La Haye's recent Christian guide, *The Act of Marriage*, claims sales of more than a million since 1976; Marabel Morgan's *The Total Woman* managed half a million; Marie Stopes's *Married Love* had sold 221,000 within five years of its publication in 1918 and was translated into French, Dutch, Swedish, German and Danish; Helena Wright's *Sex, an Outline for Young People*, first published in 1932 as *What is Sex?*, was still being revised in 1963 and was still on sale during the mid-seventies; Eustace Chesser's *Love Without Fear* sold 162,000 between 1941 and 1962, when it was reprinted. Even less well-known works by relatively unfamiliar authors managed considerable sales. Leslie Weatherhead's *The Mastery of Sex* was first published in 1931 and had sold 70,000 copies in fifteen editions by 1946; Anthony Havil's *The Technique of Sex* went through fourteen impressions in five years from 1939. Even Rennie MacAndrew's *Life Long Love*, published in 1928 by the Wales Publishing Company – a small firm in Charing Cross Road almost wholly devoted to producing books about sex – was still reprinting nearly thirty years later after twenty impressions.

Few authors of sex manuals end their days eking out a pittance doing book reviews for *Health and Efficiency*. But who does need sex manuals when sex, surely, is a matter of instinct? But is it, is it? By and large sex manual writers find it very difficult to decide, though their agonizings may be little more than the symptoms of a group which believes in one thing (instinct) and yet has a vested interest in proving the opposite (technique). Crudely, they shake down into three camps: (a) those who believe sex to be instinctive, but an instinct of such a base kind that some sort of early and regular instruction is needed as to its purpose, control and limitations; (b) those who think sex is instinctive but an instinct so buried in hypocrisy and corroded by guilt (see (a)) that some sort of instruction is needed to help people rediscover its roots; and (c) those who believe sex is not an instinct but a skill. There are those, of course, who like to keep a toe ('TOE'. See Alex Comfort: 'BIG TOE': 'A magnificent erotic instrument') in more than one camp.

You can generally sort out the first two groups by the imagery they use, drawn from animals and primitive peoples, and the way they use it. Those in the first group are in little doubt that sex is a force so electric that it threatens society itself. One hundred years ago Elizabeth Blackwell, the first woman doctor in Britain or the USA (she qualified in both places) warns that 'very grave social errors leading even to the debasement and ultimate destruction of national life flow from the hitherto rudimentary condition of our human intelligence in relation to the sexual powers'. Instruction was needed to rise above the 'grossly unchaste' standards of behaviour of 'savages'. Charles Thompson in his book *Manhood*, 1917, explains that life 'with all its possibilities of achievement, demands that we subdue to our sovereign will the *animal passion* [my italics]; not so that it shall be killed and stifled, but in order that it shall be elevated once again.' His book had been written so that his readers could learn to tame this potentially degrading force and 'know the high nobility of life'. Humans differed from animals on account of their 'directive volition' and 'the one great thing to be pressed home to us is that the racial instinct is the pride of humanity, not the shame . . . Too many regard sex as a merely personal matter, whereas it is a distinctly social affair. It is because of the selfish outlook that there exists a social evil.'

Dr Emma Drake, writing in 1901, quotes an Eastern proverb advising that it is not always a good thing to satisfy one's appetite. 'This will the beasts do whenever they find provender,' runs the saying in improbably Biblical prose. 'Man alone can say to himself, thou shalt fast because I have willed it. Appetite thus conquered maketh man king over beasts; thus is he set apart from them.' She warns her women readers – for the book is a collection of things 'a young wife ought to know' – that 'the sedentary life of many men renders them a prey to the gratification of their lower natures . . .' Such men had a 'religious duty' to exercise until such natures were tired out, and should be ostracized until they had done so. 'The sexual nature will not then dominate the finer and nobler instincts of their brain.' Van de Velde, in 1926, similarly speaks of 'obscure primitive urges' and stated as one the main objects of *Ideal Marriage* the wish 'to make the love-motive roar and suffuse and triumph over its ugly elemental foe'. Leslie Weatherhead, a former minister from Manchester, turns to the big cat family for his illustration of the darker forces of sexuality. Writing in 1931, he complains of the content of plays and novels which pandered to these instincts. 'They are a deliberate appeal to the tiger within. They bring that tiger rushing up with a roar against the bars of his cage, the bars of self-control, convention, law . . . and one day the bars may be loose or the tiger too strong and sometimes irreparable damage is done.' Later still we find Dr Eustace Chesser – a 'thorough-going liberal', according to Alex Comfort – advising us that 'to rise above the animals we must put thought, understanding and skill into love-making'. Chesser, you understand, is here to tell you how. The how, for Dr Isabel Emslie Hutton, CBE, in 1953, does not necessarily include sexual techniques practised by animals. 'The rear-entry position is practised by animals,' she tells readers, 'but is rarely used by modern man.'

It is almost unheard of in the early part of the century to find animal behaviour quoted in anything but a pejorative context, the rare exception being by way of illustration in works addressed to an adolescent audience. Thus in *Rovering to Success* Lord Baden-Powell opens his chapter on women (rock number three in 'rocks you are likely to bump on') with the example of the stag. The monarch among animals, 'a type of courage, strength and virile beauty', undergoes a 'rutting season' each autumn, he explains. 'It is those that best reserve their strength which then come out on top . . . the defeated weakling can then only sneak about trying to get what joy they can among the outcasts of the herd.' So it is with a young man. 'As with the stag, in some cases he comes out of it a strong, virile "Lord of the Herd", while in others he deteriorates and becomes the weakling or even the outcast.' Save yourself for the rutting season. No, not each autumn.

Turn to the pages of an Alex Comfort sex manual for the opposite view of animal life. His pages are littered with approving comparisons with the sexual behaviour of chimpanzees, baboons and primitives. Sex, according to Dr Comfort, is more enjoyable when thought of as natural history. Some apes use dominance and so do we, only we eroticize it. Also like us, apes will play with themselves and swing both ways. Rear entry? It is 'the other human option – for most mammals it's the only one'. He discounts the fear of modern doctors that nursemaids who masturbate young babies to soothe them end up overstimulating them. Primitives masturbate their babies, says Comfort, so it's probably harmless. The babies seem to enjoy it, anyway. From striving to subjugate and tame any 'degraded' bestial sexual instincts we land up being told we should forget the guilt trip laid on us by society over decades – centuries, even – and return to the pre-lapsarian behaviour of animals and primitives positively to study what we can rediscover about our deep-buried natural responses. Dr Helena Wright might have baulked at the notion that any act performed within the animal kingdom or Third World might have valuable lessons for us, but, writing in 1930, she is quite clear about the business of instinct. 'There can be nothing difficult about the achievement of a successful sex-life because it is the universal experience of primitive peoples and of Eastern civilization. The difference between us and them is one of approach . . . our attitude of mind towards sex in our country is unhealthy, ignorant and thoroughly unsatisfactory.' More than twenty years later, Dr Lucia Radl is still complaining that sex is 'bedevilled by prudery'.

Then there is (c). 'Sexual knowledge is not instinctive,' announces George Ryley Scott, a Fellow of the Zoological Society, in his 1947 book, *Your Sex Questions Answered*. 'That coitus is not instinctive in civilized man, whatever it may be in savage races, is proved by the fact, known to every sexologist, that there are many men and women who have no notion of how to perform the sex act.' This is, of course, a still more fireproof motive – or alibi – for the writing of sex manuals, though not one many hazard. Two writers who do are Paul Brown and Carolyn Faulder (*Treat Yourself to Sex*, 1977), who think it 'extraordinary that learning about one of the most important human activities is left entirely to chance and our friends'. Brown and Faulder pass, via the obligatory scoff at our horizontal forebears contemplating England, to characterizing sex as 'an activity . . . a shared pleasure'. They add: 'Sex is also a skill and, like any other, the better we can learn it, the more our competence will please us. Good sex does not come naturally if by "naturally" we mean that it is inborn . . . As sex is a skill, so good sex is an art . . . But, like any other art, it needs time and dedication to unravel its mysteries . . .' And preferably a book, too. But you will have got the picture.

Thus the three groups evolve, each category defining the tone and style to be adopted. Those in the first cannot emphasize enough the sobriety and detachment they bring to their task. J. Johnson Abraham, of 38 Harley Street, assures van de Velde's readers in a foreword that what follows has been presented 'soberly, scientifically, completely without a scintilla of eroticism and with a sustained note of high idealism'. Van de Velde himself describes the work as an 'accessible book of rules' but implores his public to remember 'that I have not written the preceding pages to be skimmed through – and, still less, to be read as "spicy stuff", honour and conscience forbid! – but for earnest and reverent study.' Weatherhead's foreword in 1931 by the Reverend A. Herbert Gray commends its 'high level of taste and restraint . . . from beginning to end this book is clean'. In 1901, Dr Drake professes herself reluctant to tackle the subject at all since, wrongly interpreted, 'it becomes a snare and degradation to the nobler instincts and aspirations, and lets in a legion of evil spirits which lead farther and farther away from truth and righteousness'.

Later travellers down the same road are, as you would expect, less squeamish. Alex Comfort's professed mission to liberate sex from the anxious moralizing of repressed generations led him to produce what he referred to as 'the first explicitly sexual book for the coffee table'. Animals learned sex by watching each other do it, so why not humans? Watching other couples copulating was 'not only exciting, but immensely instructive. Sex is about the only social skill we don't learn by watching.' (Yes, 'skill'; he, too, has his magnificent erotic instrument in two camps.) Instead 'grey' society has imposed ideas of modesty and privacy which implied that sex should be hidden, with the result that people had no way of checking their methods and tastes by observing others. The trouble with other sex manuals, says Comfort, is . . . well, did you ever hear of a book on football by someone who'd never seen a game in his life? That's why there's so much 'hogwash' about. 'Most of the people who have written about sexuality never saw a couple making love – probably not even Sigmund Freud; it wasn't his scene. It's a heavy thought.' As for Alex and his helpers? 'Yes, we've watched dozens of couples . . . most of the nonsense in past books simply couldn't have survived even minimal direct observation. Watching and being watched is exciting, friendly and encouraging – not intrusive or embarrassing.' Now there's another heavy thought.

But, actually, Alex and his publishers know that, exciting and instructive though watching may be, there are precious few people willing and able to bound free of society's shackles to start peeping and being peeped at in an unintrusive and unembarrassing way. So what better than a book that will do the watching for you? See

The Joy of Sex in your own living room with all the 'humour, honesty and directness' that artists Charles Raymond and Christopher Foss can bring to bear. Dr Comfort MB Ph.D, tells you it's OK, so sit back and let Raymond/Foss guide you, coffee-tablewise, on a tasteful Odyssey around clothes fetishes, oral sex, organs, masturbation, photo-sex, positions, buttocks, quickies, bondage, foursomes, gadgets, mirrors, rocking chairs, stockings, bisexuality and armpits (yes, armpits) – all this the cosy territory of *Joy* rather than the less certain hinterlands of *More Joy*. And if any of this sounds a trifle risqué for your coffee table Dr Comfort has helped you out by dressing it up as a sort of cookbook – a 'gourmet guide to lovemaking' it says on the cover, with the sections divided up into 'starters', 'main courses' and 'sauces and pickles'. You need a steady diet of sex, he wants you to know. 'The more regular sex a couple has the higher the deliberately-contrived peaks – just as the more you cook routinely, the better and more reliable banquets you can stage.'

We are now into the deluxe printings and pocket editions of *Joy* – though, as yet, no videos. But if it's videos you want, videos you can have. Write to the *Multi Media Resource Center* in San Francisco for a list of their forty (in 1977) titles. You might try *Rich and Judy*. The plot runs: 'The build-up of excitation (turn-on) stage and all four phases of the sexual response cycle are visible in this film. Note the partners' playfulness.' Or *Sun Brushed*: 'Note the aliveness and freedom of the woman in "top" position, and the integration of the orgasm with environmental sounds.' Or why not *Closing the Circle*? 'Two men and a woman bridge the sexual gap, the men relating to each other. They also reach across the generation gap; the younger man *could* be the son of the other two. Great caring and affection is shown by all three people. The woman takes the lead.' Or else try the video of the book, *Becoming Orgasmic* by Julia Heiman and Leslie and Joseph Lopiccolo. Male or female, improve your sexual growth by watching a female model 'who self-discloses her fears and concerns'.

Who needs them? Don't we all? See if any of these statements fits you:

'Sex just doesn't work for me.'
'Sex isn't what it used to be.'
'I can't get aroused, whatever my partner does.'

'I can't get a climax.'

'I'm not sure if I've ever had an orgasm.'

'I don't seem to enjoy the sex life my friends say they do.'

'I don't seem to be as good at sex as my friends say they are.'

'I just don't get turned on any more.'

'Maybe I'm getting too old.'

'I seem to have lost interest.'

'I'm worried because I know my partner doesn't enjoy it.'

'Sex is a bore.'

'Sex is marvellous but I seem to have lost the knack.'

'Sex is marvellous. Can we make it even better?'

One of them does? Then Paul Brown and Carolyn Faulder solemnly promise you that their book will help you. So you think you know it all already? Dr Chesser's 1941 figures may surprise you. 'Not one husband in twelve knows enough of the technique of love to enable him to impart and receive half the pleasure which should be derived from sexual union. Not one in a hundred has learned, by study, practice, or experience, how to gain the maximum of pleasure. The overwhelming majority of wives *never* know the supreme joy which the sex act can yield to the ideally-mated.' Chesser's dust-jacket promises to teach the 'genuine technique of love, which all can master . . . there is hardly an adult of either sex who will not find this book the key to enhanced power and joy in living'. (It adds underneath: 'The author has written this book for those who are married or about to be married and in this connection the bookseller's cooperation is requested.') Still not sure? Then see whether the authors of *Becoming Orgasmic* haven't got you in mind. 'No matter whether you're single, married, separated, divorced or widowed, under thirty or over sixty, this book is written for you.'

There *is* no escape, no excuse. These books are for us, all of us, and we need no longer feel anxious. 'There are no failures or grades . . . only learning experiences' in the *Sexual Attitude Restructuring (SAR) Guide for a Better Sex Life*, which is wholly 'non-judgemental' and feels, above all, that 'everyone has a right to a good sex life whatever form she or he desires'. There. It's your right. Take it. Let's step inside.

CONTINENCE – THE WATERLOO OF LIFE

A hundred years ago no self-respecting author of a guide to sex would dream of imparting any advice on *how to* without having first dwelled at length on *how not to*, *why not to* and – most pertinent of all – *why there was no need to*. The fashion lingered an awfully long time.

It was all to do with sperm. Which is to say it was mostly to do with morality, but the writers thought, pretended or convinced themselves that it was to do with sperm. It was also to do with energy and the extent to which energy was related to the amount of sperm spent or stored. It was, therefore, also about abstinence. But it began with nocturnal emissions, or wet dreams.

A tricky subject, wet dreams, and one on which writers could not agree. At one extreme, the 1880s saw the climax of a project which took up more than thirty years of the work of a noted London skin specialist, Dr John Laws Milton, with the publication of the twelfth and longest edition of his book, *On the Pathology and Treatment of Spermatorrhoea* (1887). Spermatorrhoea, according to Dr Milton, was the 'real, serious and sometimes obstinate disease' of involuntary seminal emissions which afflicted, in particular, middle-class men whose career structures prevented them from marrying young – 'barristers, medical men, authors, tutors, clergymen'. Anything more than one emission a month (the average in a study of three 'normal' doctors of philosophy, according to G. Stanley Hall nearly twenty-five years later, was 3.5 times a month) could lead to breathlessness, anxiety, bad digestion, brain fevers and local irritations which, when combined with masturbation and other voluntary emissions, could result in epilepsy, phthisis, insanity, paralysis and death. Large quantities of claret were a help – nothing less than a bottle a day – as was cauterization of the skin of the penis with red mercury. Better still were appliances to be fixed to the penis at night: the simplest took the form of a metal circle with fearsome spikes on the inside which would puncture the skin at the faintest stirrings. More complicated was the 'electric alarum' which gave a penis a short, sharp shock should it be unwise enough to attempt an erection during sleep.

The opposing view is taken by Dr Elizabeth Blackwell in 1884 who speaks of 'unused sperm thrown off from time to time in an entirely healthy and beneficent way by spontaneous separate individual action'. The fundamental moral standpoint is doubtless not that different from Dr Milton's, but it is reached by very different routes. To Dr Blackwell nocturnal emissions are 'a valuable aid to adult self-government' and prove that Christianity and 'the sound physiology and advanced thought of the nineteenth century' are at one. How? Because wet dreams are a method of evacuating excess sperm and thus removing the need for the 'moral degradation . . . and lustful trade in the human body' – fornication. 'Physiology condemns fornication by showing the physical arrangements which support the moral law.' Her study of physiology also leads her to believe that 'the active exercise of the intellectual and moral faculties has remarkable power of diminishing the formation of sperm and limiting the necessity of its natural removal'.

Professor Stanley Hall reports the debate to be still bubbling on in 1911, with authorities divided as to whether semen is a biologico-chemical fluid medicated by glandular secretions (the fashion for injections of the stuff was just beginning to wane) or whether it is 'dynamic and mediated by means of the nervous system and to some extent by consciousness'. In any event, the fundamental dilemma remained as to how to explain and deal – in medical, not moral, terms – with the energies that did seem in one way or another to be associated with sperm in a society utterly set against any form of pre-marital sex, let alone masturbation, beyond that relieved by nocturnal emissions. What was the nature of the sexual urge? Did it have to be given in to and what results could one expect if one did?

The first approach was to indicate the benefits that followed from seminal retention. Here is Dr L. B. Sperry in 1900. 'When the intense energies of men which seem to be exclusively of sexual origin – and which, to many, seem to be intended only for sexual expression – are not expended along those lines of activity directly intended for reproduction, they naturally find expression in deeds of gallantry, courage, heroism, philanthropy and other benevolent efforts contributive to the general good of humanity.' In this he was but echoing the sentiments of Dr Blackwell, who, on the same grounds, was against too frequent acts of sex even within marriage. 'The amount of nervous energy expended by the male in the temporary act of sexual congress is very great; out of all apparent proportion to its physical results, and is an act not to be too often repeated . . . Even in strong adult life there is a great loss of social

34

power through the squandering of adult energy, which results from any unnatural stimulus given to the passions of sex in the male.' And, as for fornication: 'the degrading habit of promiscuous intercourse, and all artificial excitements which give undue stimulation to the passion of sex, divert an immeasurable amount of mental and moral force from the great work of human advancement'.

The great work of human advancement was something no reader of this period was allowed to forget. Dr Emma Drake set out the options in 1901 after referring to the 'vast amount of vital force used in the production and expenditure of the seminal fluid'. It could be wasted – 'prostituted to the simple gratification of fleshy desire' – a route which led to weakness and depravity and probably to a world 'full of dwarfed minds and bodies . . . paranoiacs, cranks, feeble-minded, idiotic, epileptic, diseased children'. Or it could be conserved 'as legitimate control demands it to be' – which enhanced the 'mental and moral force of the man because it lifts him to a higher plane of being'.

To the Reverend J. Clark Gibson, a Wesleyan Chaplain to the Armed Forces in 1919, the battle young men have with their urges is 'the Waterloo of life'. Charles Thompson, the first editor of *Health and Efficiency*, expanded the metaphor in 1917. 'A man can become such a creature of desire that he has no control at all: he is a moral imbecile . . . naturally, it is a matter of struggle – a struggle for mastery; a man must fight his desires, fight hard and long, but each battle won means an easier victory next time. The glory of a man is to conquer his impulses.' Left uncontrolled, such impulses become sensuality – something that had 'wrecked empires and bowed nations in the dust'. And the men who had caused the downfall themselves fell first – their bodies 'enervated' by sensuality. The theory that 'there is a physiological necessity for the exercise of the reproductive organs . . . is absolutely wrong'.

This same theory, according to Chesser in 1941, derived from the Victorians and, since it did not apply to women, was surely 'part of double standards of morality'. Contradicting it was certainly something of an obsession in the early part of this century. Three of the Forces chaplains whose First World War talks on sex and purity to the troops are collected in the volume, *A Cornerstone of Reconstruction* (1919), deal with the problem at some length. The Reverend Barten Allen, an Anglican, talks of the 'horrible suggestion prevalent among men of every class that if a young man doesn't use his sexual powers from time to time he runs the risk of losing them. It is an absolute fallacy.' A man who has 'kept himself absolutely clean' until the age of thirty will, he promises, have 'children just as strong as, and perhaps stronger, than the children of a man who has been using, perhaps abusing, his sexual powers all the while.' The Reverend Gibson explains that semen is 'reabsorbed into the body, thus laying in a stock of those reserves of nervous energy, endurance and mental stamina that are to a man what reserves are to an army – the last reserves to be called upon in an emergency'. In the final lecture the Reverend A. Herbert Gray, a Presbyterian minister, tells his men: 'The longer I live, the more clearly do I see that the success or failure of a man's life very largely depends upon his learning to understand and manage his sexual nature.' Gray announces that, 'hardly a doctor with a reputation to lose' – mark that qualification carefully, please – 'would give support to the idea that there was any need to use the organs before marriage – and duly reproduces the testimony of leading doctors to prove it. 'No excuse, no requirement of nature, no overpowering necessity,' barks Sir Dyce Duckworth. Sir James Paget says he would as well prescribe theft or lying as to recommend fornication. Sir Andrew Clark goes further still: 'Necessity for fornication? Certainly not. I believe that if you keep your chastity you may live twenty years longer.' Further German authorities are cited . . . sixty doctors in Philadelphia . . . Sir Clifford Allbutt.

Marie Stopes attributed to semen more precious, rich and diverse properties than almost anybody else of the period. It is the greatest mistake, she says in *Married Love* (1918), 'to imagine that semen is something to be got rid of *frequently*'. (This, naturally, in the context of marriage.) 'All the vital energy and nerve-force involved in its ejaculation and the precious chemical substances which go towards its composition can be better utilized by being transformed into other creative work on most days of the month.' Dr Stopes thought semen could also work wonders on wives – penetrating and affecting the woman's whole organism.

The no-need-to argument went, of course, hand in hand with the barrage of moral arguments which we will look at later. But the attempt at putting forward a medically convincing case against indulgence was more resilient than you might think, as Norval

Geldenhuys demonstrates in his sex manual for Christians, *The Intimate Life* (1952). All the same arguments are rehearsed virtually straight from the Army chaplain's mouth – but forty-three years later. Pre-marital urges, he writes, are 'intended to stimulate vitality and creative power, initiative and self-sacrificing love and to develop personality. There is therefore no necessity for unmarried persons to "satisfy" this desire as in marriage. On the contrary, such "satisfaction" is extremely harmful.'

Geldenhuys's text is illustrated by a detailed plan of sluice-gates intended to show how these urges might best be sublimated, but he is a little vague when it comes actually to specifying the harm that infringement causes. 'If the sluice gate is opened prematurely (i.e. before marriage) serious destruction will be the result. The partially completed channel will be damaged, the land that could have been cultivated into something beautiful as soon as it was ready for irrigation becomes swamped, wrecking homes and ruining lives.' He is a little more direct on the subject of unused sperm. 'Recent research shows' – the three favourite words in the sex manual author's lexicon – 'that it is absorbed by the body, invigorating the person concerned with new power, initiative and enterprise.'

A similar vagueness tends to afflict writers who find themselves troubled by problems of consistency once they stray into the question of continence within marriage. William Sadler, writing in 1952, declares such a thing 'a crime against the nervous system'. Yet Sadler is pretty adamant that the nervous system can withstand any amount of continence on the part of the unmarried, leading, at worst – and in people already nervously unstable – to neurosis. He adds: 'a study of the happiness of married couples indicates that those who indulge in such relations are definitely sacrificing some of their chances for tranquility and happiness after marriage'.

Leslie Weatherhead quotes approvingly from a no-need-to article about pre-marital sex from the December 1927 *Journal of Social Hygiene* before advising wives not to refuse their husbands sex because of the 'powerful source of energy still directed to intercourse and its primaeval goal'. Worse still was abstinence, which 'so often leads to strain, friction, irritability and bad temper'. Weatherhead duly attempts an explanation of the transfiguration in the sex urge – once tamable, now inexorable –

brought about by marriage. 'Continence outside marriage is a very different thing from abstinence when, night after night, propinquity stimulates passionate desire which is unexpressed. It is one thing to do without food when in a desert. To be taken to the grill-room where desire is stimulated unbearably and still not be allowed food is a form of torture.'

Thus, with one or two hardy exceptions, the debate muddles itself into the distance. Especially muddled will be those seeking to lead a long life, torn between Sir Andrew Clark's offer of another twenty years in exchange for continence and Dr Alex Comfort's claim that regular sex preserves bodily functions long into old age: 'hormone levels depend on it; so, therefore, do looks and vigour'.

And as for sperm, with which it all began, it shed its almost mystical attributes somewhere along the way. Could the once mysterious vital force ever be more mundanely regarded than by Alex Comfort in warning: 'It's hard to get out of furnishings . . . pick semen-proof furniture'? The answer, for once, is yes. The *Complete Book of Love* tells us it's non-fattening.

3

The Solitary Vice

Onan, brother of Er, has had a very raw deal from history. There is nothing to suggest he ever played with himself but merely – according to Genesis – practised *coitus interruptus* with his late brother's widow. The Lord slew him for his pains, and his posthumous fate has been to be credited for the better part of three centuries with the invention of masturbation.

It may seem strange to come across the mention of such a practice in a discussion of sex manuals, but only to those who have never read one. There is scarcely a book of sex advice that does not dwell at some – and sometimes extraordinary – length on onanism or, as we are now encouraged to know it, 'self-pleasuring' or 'finding out alone'. Of all the whoppers ever told about sex onanism is surely the greatest. Starting early in the eighteenth century and lasting well into the second half of the twentieth a succession of doctors, psychiatrists, clergymen and teachers thundered home the inevitable biological and mental consequences of masturbating. If a hundredth of the diseases it was said to cause were really linked with the act the entire Western world would long ago have been wholly populated by blind, impotent, bald, dwarf, epileptic cowards. And that would be just the humans. For, as Professor G. Stanley Hall notes in 1911, 'we have many and well-attested cases of this perversion's prevalence among monkeys, dogs, blood stallions, elephants, turkeys, etc.'. Yes, even turkeys. Don't tell Bernard Matthews.

Since most studies – from Tissot, one of the very first scaremongerers, right through to the 1980s – have found that the overwhelming majority of people have masturbated at some stage in their lives it is a wonder that the propaganda was so powerful and successful for so long. One can only suppose that the guilt and terror induced in so many people prevented the sort of common-place discussion of the habit which would have rapidly established that the experts were, indeed, fibbing their hearts out.

That the early eighteenth-century author of *Onania, or the Heinous Sin of Self-Pollution*, should have chosen thus to besmirch the name of Onan was doubtless to impress upon the public the awesome link between the spilling of seed and Biblical slaying. The term 'onanism' was still in use in sex manuals in the mid-1960s, more than 250 years after it was first coined, though it has gone under several aliases in the past hundred years alone. It has also been utterly anonymous in the hands of writers who simply could not bring themselves to mention any name at all. Thus G. H. Darwin, in suggesting that it might be responsible for leucorrhoea, a variety of thrush, refers to it in 1884 simply as a practice 'which can only be vaguely alluded to, which affects unmarried women chiefly, but which is known to the student of mental diseases as one of the most terrible of those hidden ulcers, which eat into the health of both sexes, and beneath the fair-seeming surface of society, are destroying manliness, womanhood, and all that renders life worth living'. At least, one assumes that this is what he is talking about.

Dr Elizabeth Blackwell, in the same year, refers to it variously as masturbation, self-abuse and the 'Solitary Vice', while Dr Emma Drake, at the turn of the century, can only bear to talk of 'this dangerous shoal, this evil, this secret vice'. Similarly, the Reverend the Honourable E. Lyttelton, a future headmaster of Eton, writing in 1900, talks only of 'self-defilement' and 'the stormy physical trial' faced by adolescents – even though he devotes no fewer than twenty-nine of his 117 pages to the subject. Hall, Professor of Psychology and Pedagogy at Clark University, refers to it in 1911 as 'self-abuse . . . the scourge of the human race . . . a vice . . . a perversion . . . an evil . . . this insidious disease . . . an influence that seems to spring from the Prince of Darkness . . .' Van de Velde speaks of 'ipsatresses', and as late as 1925 'A Physician', the anonymous author of *For Men Only*, can give no name to what he terms 'a hidden evil, like a hidden ulcer'. In apocalyptic tones he talks of 'an evil in our midst which if persisted in will sap the energy and wreck the manhood of any youth'. He excuses himself by explaining that 'it is not easy to describe or discuss any of these secret habits and vices without giving offence, indeed it is so extremely difficult that some may regard it as impossible'. In his case, certainly.

The most striking example of this habit that dared not speak its

THE SOLITARY VICE

name comes during the course of one of the four Great War
lectures to the Forces by chaplains – in this example the
Reverend A. Herbert Gray, a Presbyterian, who manages to
recite an entire cautionary story about the dire consequences of
the act without ever stating what the act is. 'It is the story of a
man who while he was still young found that his sight was
beginning to fail and therefore went to consult a doctor. After
examining him, the doctor said: "Young man, if you do not
change your way of life you will be blind in six months." It was a
lovely day in summer and the sunshine was streaming in at the
window. When the young man had heard his doctor's verdict he
turned to the window and said: "Then, farewell light, fair light,
for I cannot give up my sin." Does it not seem to you that there
was something tragically shameful in such bondage to a bodily
passion? Do you not feel that the man was surrendering his
essential manhood?'

Since those days masturbation has, of course, become obligatory
– prescribed by the sex professionals who have meanwhile set to
work 'to void the negative overtones' of the language of yesteryear.
'J', the author of *The Sensuous Woman* (1972), complains that
' "masturbation" is an awkward, ugly, socially unutterable word
for one of the most gratifying human experiences'. The 1975 *Sexual
Attitude Restructing (SAR) Guide* has us exorcising the past by
reciting all the names it can think of without judgemental
overtones: 'self-sexuality, self-pleasuring, autoeroticism, sex
without a partner, playing with yourself, whacking off, diddling,
fiddling, twiddling yourself, jacking off and [since this is
California] jilling off'.

So much for the names; what about (in pre-Jack and Jill days)
the causes? Hall comes up with a reasonably comprehensive list:
'consumptive heredity . . . a long convalescence, piles, habitual
constipation, irritating urinal deposit, malformation of the organs,
idleness and laziness, weakness of the will and doubtless heredity'
were among the more general aetiological roles. 'Among the
external causes', continues Prof. Hall, 'are springtime, which is a
peculiarly dangerous season, warm climates, improper clothes,
rich food, indigestion, mental overwork, nervousness, habits of
defective cleanliness, especially of a local kind, prolonged sitting or
standing, too monotonous walking, sitting cross-legged, spanking,
late rising, petting and indulgence, corsets that produce stagnation

or hyperemia of blood in the lower part of the body and too great straining of the memory.' You think Prof. Hall has finished? He has not. 'Prominent among predisposing causes are often placed erotic reading, pictures, and theatrical presentations.' Some authorities, he says, have demanded an expurgated Bible and dictionaries. 'Others would banish the *Odes* of Horace, the *Satires* of Juvenal, to say nothing of Martial and Terence, and forbid ballets. Certain drugs, like phosphorus, cocaine, opium, camphor, and inhalation of oxygen, are now known to have stimulating effect, while others, like digitalis, saltpetre, arsenic, have an opposite effect.' Other authorities 'protest against trouser-pockets for boys, as do others against feather-beds, while even horseback riding and the bicycle have been placed under the ban . . . indulgence in intoxicating drink without doubt predisposes to it, as does any physical or psychic difficulty in access to closets, solitude, certain perfumes, overeating, fondling fur, and rocking chairs'.

Do not, please, be tempted into imagining that this list is exhaustive. Gallichan, in 1919, adds: 'lying in too warm beds, idly day-dreaming . . . the sedentary life lived by many girls. It has been proved that the treadle sewing machine produces sex excitement in some women . . . Overheated rooms, lounging, lack of interest and amusements and reading inflammatory love stories.' Marie Stopes goes for the hereditary aspects. 'Mothers whose natural desire for union had been denied, and mothers who are congenitally frigid rather tend to reproduce children with unbalanced sex-feeling liable to yield to self-abuse.' Van de Velde takes a severe line against most forms of transport: 'Men may experience an erection while on horseback, or driving in a carriage or travelling by train; more rarely, perhaps while motoring or bicycling . . . I have known ipsatresses who lamented to me that journeys *drove* them to indulge in a habit their minds resisted and disapproved.'

Little wonder, with almost any daily activity liable to provoke onanism, that the authors of advice on sexual matters think it right to warn parents of the symptoms in terms foreshadowing 1960s' magazine features on how to tell if your child smoked pot. Dr Drake advises mothers to be on the look-out for a child that is 'listless, and preferring solitude than companionship, averse to exercise, averted look, nervous, constipated, hypochondriacal, restless in sleep, . . . pain in the back and lower extremities in the morning, hands cold and clammy; . . . another diagnostic symptom is this: the body emits a peculiar, disagreeable smell, and there is emaciation.' 'A Physician' produces an even more certain test in 1925. 'There is often one way in which the existence of it shows itself in a lad, and that is in the character of what he draws or writes. This often tends to be rough sketches of private parts and school masters should have an alert eye for any evidence of anything of this nature.'

The Reverend the Honourable E. Lyttelton thinks matters less clear-cut. 'One of the symptoms by which a parent may be guided is the strength of the appetite for food at an early age, before bodily growth begins to be rapid . . . but excepting in the one symptom . . . I doubt if there are any indications which will enable even an experienced man to be certain that a boy is not beginning to contract the habit. In the early stages no safe inferences can be drawn from the expression or demeanour . . . There is something extraordinarily stealthy and uncertain about the attacks of this particular foe . . . emotional and sometimes precociously religious boys are found to be in sad trouble from it. But on the whole there is no rule, and the best plan is to definitely ask the question.'

Those who do ask the question receive alarming answers. Tissot, in 1759, found that every single pupil in the *lycée* he investigated was guilty. Benseman found it extraordinarily prevalent in English schools. Dr Seerley, of Springfield, Mass., discovered in the early part of the century that, of 125 academic students, only eight could convince him that they had never indulged. Gallichan, in 1919, cites various authorities to prove that women and girls did it more than their male counterparts while Weatherhead in 1931 says that virtually all men and 80 per cent of women have been guilty.

If one missed the tell-tale symptoms one could but wait for the results to start manifesting themselves. Some were vaguer than others. Dr Elizabeth Blackwell does not tell how she spots the habit in patients in the 1880s – merely that it can 'destroy the body'. She illustrates her claim with a tale of 'an intelligent and pious' Sunday School teacher 'dying from the effects of this inveterate habit'. Hall, as ever, offers wholesale the numerous physical effects: 'subjective light sensations, optical cramps, perhaps Basedow's disease (goitre), intensification of the patellar reflex, weak sluggishness of heart action and circulation seen in cold extremities, purple and dry skin, lassitude and flaccidity, clammy hands,

anaemic complexion, dry cough and many digestive perversions
. . . listlessness and frigidity . . . a predisposition to convulsions . . .
early signs of decrepitude and senescence. Grey hairs, and
especially baldness, a stooping and enfeebled gait, marks of early
caducity which may crop out in retina, in cochlea, in the muscular
or nervous system, in the stomach . . . it finally ends in complete
sterility.' Baden-Powell warns his would-be Rovers: 'it checks
semen getting its full chance of making you the strong manly man
you would otherwise be. You are throwing away the seed that has
been handed down to you as a trust instead of keeping it and
ripening it for bringing a son to you later on.'

Later writers are more modest in the range of afflictions they
dare to pin on masturbation, though we still find Dr Lucia Radl
warning in 1953 that 'boys who practise masturbation will, when
they mature and marry, have great difficulty achieving the self-
control necessary to produce the woman's orgasm . . . in girls it
can of course prove a handicap in achieving sexual gratification.'
No subject would be wholly complete without a chirpy contribution from Dr Gilbert Oakley. Ever an original, he advances the
theory that in the teenage boy masturbation actually 'helps him
clear his face of adolescent spots and blemishes [and] purifies his
blood stream'. It is only later in life that the damage begins. He
states (1963, remember) that repeated self-abuse leads to 'shaking
limbs . . . poisoning of the blood stream . . . impotence . . . priap-
ism . . . neurasthenia and storrhoea . . . and may cause irigendi'
(the inability to get an erection). Why, it even leads to our old
friend spermatorrhoea because, Dr Oakley argues, the ejaculation
mechanism becomes worn out. Fortunately, he reassures us, 'this
occurs only with onanists who commit the act many times in a
day.'

This is only the beginning, though; for more insidious still are
the mental and moral effects. Dr Drake records in 1901 that 'some
of the terrible results are epilepsy, idiocy, catalepsy and insanity. It
has been discovered that out of 800 cases of insanity in the New
York State Insane Asylum there were 107 addicted to this
practice.' Prof. Hall, not to be outdone, lists the authorities for
asserting that the act causes a form of insanity whose symptoms
are 'cerebral anaemia . . . alternating spells of gluttony and
anorexia, cowardice, suspecting the purity of all others, avoidance
of rough, manly sports, neglect of toilet and dress, spells of sulks

and cruelty', to name but a few. Hall himself cites 'psychic impotence, lying, secretiveness and hypocrisy, cowardice, timidity, egoism and frivolity. The power of pity and sympathy is often almost extinguished ... The masturbator's heart, so often discussed, is weak like his voice.'

Walter Gallichan argues in 1919 that the act leads to a distaste for marriage since it is 'apt to foster misogny in man and misanthropy in women ... some masturbators seem incapable of falling in love in a natural manner.' Men become 'blasé and cynical' and women adopt a false modesty. The Reverend A. Herbert Gray in the same year tells the troops that playing with themselves 'leads to ... moral weakness ... it is, in a sense, man's castration of himself, the depriving of himself, by his own act, of all manly attributes and powers, leaving himself feeble in body, futile in mind'. 'A Physician' in 1925 presents his own clammy-handed onanists for scrutiny: 'its victims live solitary lives; they shun the society of their fellows and cannot enter into the amusement and games of youth; they lose the frank direct look of manly youth.'

But we should not forget Dr Oakley, who is quite specific about the activities of the self-abuser. Exaggerated fantasies while masturbating may lead boys to attack girls ... or one may 'lurk in a woodside, lying in wait for a girl to pass by, and then will expose himself to her in an unhappy and desperate attempt to seek a partner with whom to share his sexual excitement.' More particularly still: 'We meet the victim to prolonged self-abuse, the victim to wilful deprivation of normal sex instincts, in the woman ever in search of a "cause" to which to attach herself', the man for ever promoting strikes among his fellow workers, the girl 'dedicated to her work' whatever it might be, the youth determined to be the leader of the 'movement', the men with 'messages' to give to the world, the soap-box fanatics on the street corners. The spinster with all her maternal instincts centred upon keeping and caring for countless cats, the woman of substance donating large sums to various charities, the man behind the imposing beard, the artist with the impossible 'abstract' canvases. Down to the shoplifters, the pill takers, the petty pilferers, the men 'agin the law'. Truly, 'Sex without the "X"'.

Rare are the early writers candid enough to confess to the lack of any evidence as to the alleged mental and physical ravages. As early as 1884 Dr Blackwell quotes – though certainly does not endorse – a medical colleague who argues: 'medically speaking it is of no consequence whatever. Mind I say MEDICALLY, not morally speaking.' Even the more enlightened authors generally advance an argument that runs: it won't do any harm, but what with the way that the rest of society views it you'll end up hating yourself and feeling so guilty that these feelings in themselves will do damage. Thus Gallichan: 'Victims who have been told that they will become lunatics have actually lost their reason through dread alone. Dr Savage and other authorities mention suicide as a result.' Or Leslie Weatherhead, who dismisses most previous writings as 'vulgar nonsense' and yet warns that shame and self-loathing may well cause 'all sorts of pathological mental conditions'. Baden-Powell tells his Rovers that their self-respect will be knocked out: 'You are doing a thing that you dare not mention to your parents or sisters; YOU ARE ASHAMED; it is something low and unmanly. A man who is ashamed is no longer a man; he becomes a conscious sneak.' Helena Wright, a liberal-minded feminist, deplores in 1963 the habit's predisposition to 'secrecy and a desire to shun society'. It is an 'anti-social habit' which has a 'bad effect on thought-atmosphere' and one which can lead to difficulties in performing the 'normal act' of intercourse in marriage. Even Tim and Beverly LaHaye, writing in 1976, complain that the modern encouragement of sex 'does not take into account . . . the guilt that almost always follows it'.

So what is to be done? With such a menacing variety of masturbatory causes around, prodigious feats of vigilance are demanded of parents, teachers and vicars by way of precautions. 'Mothers need to be Argus-eyed,' warns Dr Drake in 1901. 'If there is the slightest tendency in your children to secret vice, do not allow them to sleep together in the same bed . . . keep from their food all that is stimulating, such as coffee, pepper, spices, pickles . . . give them a quick sponge bath of salt and water (tepid) . . . in the morning a shower bath of cool water. Children, until they are old enough to be trusted, should not be out from under their mother's watchful eye. Be careful . . . guard what they read . . . and you will be rewarded with strong, pure boys and girls who can look into your eyes candidly and say, "Mamma, I am free from this habit which leads to so much misery." '

But when are they old enough to be trusted? Most sex manual writers of this school address themselves to adolescents at the very least and, more usually, young men and women in their twenties troubled by urges and yet too young or with too little by way of savings to get married. 'A Physician' recommends plentiful exercise as the answer, 'for sheer physical fatigue forbids the mind to dally with the alluring and dangerous topic of sex'. Ultimately, though, it is up to the young man himself. 'No drugs will "cure it", nor will any vaunted treatment by means of electricity applied in any form.'

Hall likewise has little faith in such 'cures' – bromide, ergot, lupin, blistering, clitoridectomy – nor any of the numerous mechanical appliances registered at the Washington Patent Office. 'Regimen rather than special treatment' is what he recommends. 'Work reduces temptation and so does early rising, while excessive mental or physical effort easily fatigues before the power of resistance is acquired. Good music is a moral tonic.' He is in favour of circumcision and of close attention to dress: 'Trousers should not be too highly drawn up by suspenders, as boys are so prone to do, but should be left loose and lax. They should be made ample, despite fashions often unhygienic . . . Underpants for both sexes should be loose and well cut away, and postures, automisms and acts that cause friction should be discouraged. Too great thickness of garments here is harmful in another way, for coolness is no less essential. Pockets should be placed well to the side and not too deep, and should not be kept too full, while habitually keeping the hands in the pockets should be discouraged.'

Hall further recommends underpants which open only at the sides and cool clothing for cold weather. 'Rooms, too, should not be kept too warm . . . Beds should be rather hard and the covering should be light, because too much not only produces excessive heat, but presses upon the body and reduces the effectiveness of circulatory and respiratory processes. Too soft a bed develops a diathesis of sensuous luxury and tempts to remain too long after awakening, and just this hour is probably the most dangerous time of all. The habit of retiring and rising early is by far the best for eyes and nerves as well as for morals. One or more windows should always be open at night in the sleeping room of adolescents, and the temperature kept as low as is compatible with health. Each should have at least a bed, if not a room to himself, but it should not be too remote and not too secluded from adult observation.' One sees in his words the foundation of generations of boarding school life – no hands in pockets, baggy grey flannels, hard mattresses, chill dormitories – pillars of which survive to this day.

More than thirty-five years later (1947) Ryley Scott concentrates on much the same sort of thing – loose trousers, night-shirts 'instead of the fashionable trousers . . . children should not be allowed to have their breakfast in bed, nor to lie awake reading either at night or in the morning.' The Reverend A. Herbert Gray (1919) advises plenty of exercise and 'total abstinence from evil thoughts; cultivate a hobby – read, sing, do anything to fill the mind with clean things'.

The other great source of deliverance from the affliction has traditionally been prayer. Modern Christian sex and marriage manuals are in some difficulty over the subject since, search as the authors will, they can find nothing in the Bible which actually condemns masturbation. The best anyone can manage is Tim and Beverly LaHaye's reading of I Cor. 7:5 ('Defraud ye not one the other, except it be with consent for a time') which, to Tim and Beverly, suggests an instruction to husbands not to cheat on their wives by playing with themselves. 'Masturbation', they announce, 'is a thief of love.' A Christian's cure method outlined by the Reverend Barrington O. Burrell in *Love, Sex and Marriage* (1983) involves a programme of sublimation: 'At the first sign of temptation occupy yourself at once with something, i.e. a crossword or jigsaw puzzle . . . try to memorize a verse of the Scripture you thought you had forgotten . . . if the temptation is usually whilst in the bath, then try to sing a song or meditate on something.' Burrell also recommends going to bed mechanically repeating a phrase such as: 'This habit is losing its hold on me.'

The Reverend Barry Chant (1977) thinks masturbation not actually physically harmful but since it is, he says, virtually impossible to practise it without thinking lustful thoughts, the act is 'definitely sinful'. In this he is echoing Leslie Weatherhead's musings of forty-six years earlier: 'We cannot help the callers who come to the doorstep and even ring the bell. We can help saying "come into the living room and make yourselves at home." Masturbation becomes sinful when such thoughts are DELIBER-ATELY ENTERTAINED.'

How mortal a sin is it? To the Catholics (*New Catholic Encyclopaedia*, 1967) it is 'a serious sin that will keep one from heaven' – apparently relying on mention of the 'covetous' who will never inherit the kingdom of God in I Cor. 6:10. Barry Chant and Leslie Weatherhead take a more shirtsleeves view. No worse than

losing your temper, says Leslie. Don't, says Barry, view it as a
terrible source of guilt: 'You haven't ruined everything. Granted,
you may have disappointed yourself and God [but] to fail may be
compared to falling in the mud. To condemn yourself and live in
misery over your failure is like staying in the mud. Get up, man.'
Barry has an old-fashioned faith in women.

But, unnoticed by Barrington and Barry, the tide has turned. 'It
isn't a bit evil, and don't let anyone tell you it is,' chirrups 'J',
author of *The Sensuous Woman* in 1970, as she embarks on a detailed
explanation of the best and latest techniques ('you must train like
an athlete for the act of love'). A sin? But we have Alex Comfort
speaking of the 'divine gift of lechery' in connection with
masturbation. Guilt? Harvey Gochros and Joel Fisher have some
advice for 1980s' parents who worry: 'Kids need a sexual outlet,
too, and all you can do is lay a guilt trip on your son or daughter if
you bug him or her about masturbating.' Unnecessary? Listen to
Paul Brown and Carolyn Faulder: 'As a means of learning about
our own body, and what gives pleasure . . . it is essential to our full
sexual realization.' But what if you catch your daughter actually in
the act? 'The answer is, rejoice and be exceedingly glad that she's
learning a skill,' advises Dr Comfort. 'Say it's something she'll be
able to enjoy all her life, a practice for adult lovemaking and the
only way to learn her own responses.' And the other way round – if
you're a teenager and a parent catches you? 'If you should be
interrupted and whoever it is that disturbs you looks horrified, try
to figure out why they're horrified,' thinks Jane Cousins in *Make it
Happy* (1978).

Won't it cause harm? Quite the contrary. Joseph Nowinski
(1976) talks of 'evidence to suggest that a total abstinence of any
sexual outlet for a prolonged period of time can lead to prostate
problems, loss of sexual interest and erection difficulties in men,
and to vaginal congestion and even shrinking of the vagina in
women. In men, a lack of masturbation can also contribute to a
tendency to ejaculate quickly.' Doctors don't agree, surely? But
here are three of them – the authors of *The Complete Book of Love and
Sex* (1983): 'Learning to masturbate bears the same relation to
intercourse as does learning to speak to conversation . . . as well as
being a form of sexual training, masturbation, or rather its
associated fantasies, helps to bring images of the bodies of the
opposite sex and of intercourse with them to mind, especially in the

young. This is a learning process and is a kind of sexual rehearsal for the adolescent.' But, all the same, the whole subject's a bit debatable, isn't it? 'Whether to masturbate is academic by now,' says Helen Gurley Brown in 1983. 'All the women I discuss these things with say they wouldn't have survived without it and STILL couldn't.'

You can't survive without it now; you were lucky to survive with it before. The only anxiety today is over what kind of half-baked sex life you can expect if you don't find out alone and whether anyway by then your organs will not have shrivelled to a frozen pea. There is one clincher: it is your *right* to find out alone: a 'natural right', says Nowinski; 'a right to take time to enjoy yourself,' say Gochros and Fisher. 'How would you feel if you were told that it was wrong to make yourself laugh or that it was right only if your partner wasn't there to tell you a joke? You would probably think this was ridiculous and would feel restricted and angry. It would be a ridiculous rule and you wouldn't obey it. The same thing applies to masturbation.'

So let's do it. But, who do you want to do it with? The basics are more or less the same, but there are numerous different approaches: Berlitz, Linguaphone, plus three dozen more. Take the Nowinski Method. Pupils begin with a bath or shower and a big tube of body lotion. They learn the 'shuttle' technique of fantasizing. The prospectus encourages students to 'approach fantasizing as a skill that you can develop with practice'. There is some homework involved, in particular keeping a 'Sexual Fantasy Record' in which pupils record any and all sexual thoughts that pop up each day for a week. There is also a certain amount of background reading, including men's magazines and sex novels. The course moves on to the 'letting go alone' stage in which pupils are encouraged to lie on a bed and 'begin to moan, groan' or say something to express their feelings. Phrases are suggested. 'Say things like: "Oh! Wow!" ' It is recommended that this exercise be repeated many times, perhaps twice a week.

The Gochros–Fisher school also begins with a bath or shower, followed by fantasy skill development during which pupils are encouraged to 'role play intense ecstasy, tossing your head from side to side and moaning and groaning'. Male pupils are urged to 'rediscover their penises'. There is some basic instruction in the lay-out of the sexual muscles and first steps in the use of the vibrator, lubricants, feathers, fur, perfumes, coloured lights and mirrors. Variety is the key-note of the Gochros–Fisher method, with different suggested locations, such as during a coffee break at work or on a swing. As with Nowinski there is a certain amount of prepared work, which may take the form of a written exercise or dictation into a tape-recorder.

The Brown–Faulder course comes as a prelude to later non-genital sensate focus classes. A bath is followed by an extended self-pleasuring period during which pupils are urged to follow their imagination wherever it leads them. The authors offer this guarantee: 'Never again need you experience sexual frustration.'

Followers of the popular 'J' school method are warned in advance that the course does require a certain degree of commitment and pupils are advised: 'Set aside several hours a week for masturbation so your new response pattern will become a stable one.' Lessons are given in vibrator, hand, water and 'variant' massage – the latter involving a variety of suggested objects. The course promises to help pupils learn a 'multiple-orgasm pattern' and comes with the author's personal recommendation: 'I'm completely sold on the value of masturbation to teach your body to be sexually responsive. It worked for me and for many other women.'

Another popular course is the *SAR* self-help programme, which is also available with Sexological exam video tapes showing masturbation in action. Pupils are asked to fill in an extensive questionnaire with a partner or friend and to keep a daily journal of their reactions and self-sexuality. A comprehensive reading list accompanies the course material, which is intended 'to help people understand the normalcy of masturbation'. Pupils are expected to take at least an hour over each exercise and are gradually helped to a 'realistic objectification of the range of behaviour'.

There is the occasional note of caution in amongst all this lot. 'J' advises periodic abstention 'after doing *lots* of masturbating – you get *too* preoccupied'. Jane Cousins adds a brief footnote: 'You don't *have* to masturbate if you don't want to.' And Sheila Kitzinger – who includes explicit photographs of a woman finding-out-alone-but-for-the-cameraman – writes (1983): 'My overriding impression is that women not only feel guilty about masturbation but now also feel guilty about being guilty . . . Most of us probably feel we have worked out our own ideas about masturbation and that it is a normal part of sexual experience. But for some it isn't easy and being instructed to be free makes them feel worse than ever.' Ms Kitzinger's readers who feel that way are advised to skip pages 67–91. You have it: the Kitzinger School of Self-Discovery.

4

Jane... Françoise... Helen... Jackie......
Lizzie.. Sue... bird at Henderson's party...
Alice... Gilly... Helga... Maureen ....
...Tamsin... Rosa... Carol... Susie... Jean...
Gina... Robyn... Ron's secretary... Sally...
Gemma... Lyn... Virginia... Mary.....
Suzanne... Wendy... Claire ....
Annie... Pauline... Sophie......

Extra-marital Sex:
The Dirt in the Gutter beside
the Path of Life

The restrained pale blue dust-jacket of Dr Eustace Chesser's *Love Without Fear* (1941) carries an appeal to retailers: 'The author has written this book for those who are married or about to be married, and in this connection the bookseller's cooperation is requested.' Similarly, the biological diagrams in Anthony Havil's book, *Toward a Better Understanding of Sexual Relationships* (1939), are in a sealed section at the back 'because it is not intended that the illustrations should be suitable for display . . . they are of interest only to the serious reader'. The serious reader was, of course, a married reader or else one on the brink of marriage. This sort of knowledge couldn't be allowed to fall into the wrong hands. Extra-marital sex was dangerous ground. 'The dirt in the gutter beside the path of life,' as the Reverend Gibson put it in 1919.

But booksellers were not wholly to be depended upon to weed out serious readers from the less serious variety and so something needed to be said to discourage premature experimentation amongst those who had not already been convinced by the argument that there was simply no need to do what they apparently had in mind.

Just as the onanophobics enlisted medicine to their cause, so religion and civic duty were harnessed in the fight for pre-marital chastity. In contrast with onanism there was no shortage of Biblical texts with which to prove that sex before marriage was what the Reverend Barrington O. Burrell calls 'the devil's territory'. Play around before you're hitched and you won't inherit the kingdom of God, Tim and Beverly LaHaye caution their readers (Gal. 5:19–21 and 1 Cor. 6:9), while the Reverend Burrell gleefully skates through some of the unhappy experiences of those who have journeyed across this diabolic land – Samson's downfall through fornication . . . Mosaic stonings to death . . . priests' daughters burned alive.

Which is not to say that both doctors and clergymen were not above flourishing the odd *soupçon* of evidence as to the likely medical effects of intercourse outside its acceptable parameters. Risk of physical or mental ill-effects thus becomes Reason Number One to stay pure. Dr Elizabeth Blackwell is quite clear in 1884 that fornication produces 'moral degradation and physical disease', quite apart from the fact that 'lustful trade in the human body is a grave social crime'. Almost 100 years later, in 1983, the Reverend Burrell advises that the 'guilt-scars in one's personality' that follow on from pre-marital sex can lead to insanity: 'Many young people consequently end up in a mental institution.' Dr Sperry warns in 1900 that intimacy during engagement endangers to some extent not only moral character but 'physical and mental development as well . . . Sexuality is almost certain to be overstimulated, amorousness unduly cultivated and lust developed and made chronic.' Sperry is in a little difficulty as to the actual symptoms that one could expect, but slides instead into a blur of medico-commercial terminology: 'It is a sad fact that by undue familiarity [and Sperry does not even necessarily include the 'real act' in this] the delicate bloom of purity is brushed from the cheek of character; the young woman, though she remain a virgin, is soiled and mussed by overmuch handling; she becomes "shop-worn" or "second-hand goods" and, by the world's best judges, is invoiced at a discount.' A similar fudging of medicine and economics is indulged in by the Reverend Gibson, who warns that the fornicator 'must pay for sexual excesses and pay in the coinage that [Nature] will demand. He must pay in loss of memory, in undermined nervous system, in weakening intellect and in vitiated willpower.' One came across men who were 'too old at 40 . . . not through age but because at 40 years of age Nature sometimes hands in the bill that a man has totted up by years of sexual indiscipline and unchastity, and when the bill is prosecuted the debtor is bankrupt and cannot pay. Memory is gone, mind is weakened and their whole manhood is discounted.' Already we are moving imperceptibly into Reason Number Two to stay pure – Manliness; but we must linger a little while with medicine to consider its most potent manifestation (pregnancy apart) – VD.

This was, of course, by no means a spurious argument in the battle for purity – the Royal Commission on Venereal Disease in 1919 found 450,000 syphilitics in London alone. The spread of the disease during the First World War forced public discussion of something that was still widely considered taboo. The Reverend B. W. Allen tells his troops in his sample lecture: 'I don't think that I have ever had a more unpleasant task than that which I have today. I have to speak on the social and moral aspects of VD. It is an absolutely disgusting subject to speak about.' Both his colleague, the Reverend J. Wallett, and Lord Baden-Powell pay tribute to a play dealing with the subject, Eugene Brieux's *Damaged Goods* (*Les Avaries*), which, after a fifteen-year ban, was eventually produced in London in March 1917 and ran for nearly 300 performances.

Baden-Powell warns that VD is easily caught from kisses or drinking from a cup used by an infected person. Syphilis could also be transmitted by saliva on a pipe stem, gonorrhoea by an 'infected towel'. 'The danger is not one which anyone will joke about once he knows the depth of it, is it?' demands Baden-Powell. 'Remember, too, that a man who has once been infected, even though apparently cured, is liable to carry the germ of the disease in him for years, and later on to pass it on to his wife and future children; and this makes it a crime on his part to marry, for he will ruin innocent lives through his own folly.'

The Alliance of Honour, alarmed by the 'eruption of impurity' they saw about them, issued posters in the Great War warning men that 'the only certain protection against venereal disease is purity and self-control'. This was only just true. Chemical preparations based on mercury, borated Vaseline and antiseptics did offer some protection, but even at the height of the war it was thought more effective to frighten troops than equip them with either the requisite knowledge or the prophylactic drugs. Omitted from decades of books was any hint that there might be preventive steps – other than abstinence – that could be taken. Both during and after the war doctors thrashed out in the medical press the morality of sharing the information about preventative methods with the general public. T. Dobson Poole wrote to the BMJ in 1922: 'We are therefore left with only one safe method – discretion – and our only method is fear . . . The fear of a broken spirit, the clipped wings shutting off the vista of future happiness, sinks more into the heart of youth than any amount of proffered mythical fruit of modern towers of Babel.'

The fear did sink deep, and took roots, so that as late as 1947, well into the antibiotic age, no fewer than fifty-five of the questions about sex in George Ryley Scott's *Your Sex Questions Answered* are anxious inquiries about sexual diseases – can I catch it by kissing, from public lavatories, off my doctor or dentist? – while Dr Isabel Emslie Hutton's *The Hygiene of Marriage* (1953) carries photographs of grotesque hunched and shrivelled victims of venereal disease. (Compare and contrast *The Sensuous Woman* by 'J' (1970): 'The risks [of getting VD] aren't adequate reasons for you to deprive yourself of a wonderful sex life . . . and all are correctable. You're in greater danger driving your car to the supermarket.')

And so to Manliness, a subtler approach for those who would not simply be scared off by medicine. Manliness resulted from chivalry – one of Baden-Powell's paddles as his Rovers manoeuvred their canoes around the rock of Woman. Chivalry involved 'putting woman on a pedestal' for, as Baden-Powell explained, 'a man who has this chivalry and respect for women could never lower himself to behave like a beast . . . a man without chivalry is no man.' It was, of course, up to the man 'to give the lead'. The First World War troops were asked to sign a pledge card, resolving 'by God's grace always to be able to look my mother or sister, my wife or my sweetheart, in the face and to have in my memory no dark night that I would hide from her. I pray that on my marriage I may know that I have played the man and acted fairly and that I give the same gift of spotless purity which I hope to receive.' The Reverend J. Wallett urges a man to think of his future wife, wherever she may be, 'keeping herself pure and upright, and perhaps also a little aloof, dreaming rosy dreams of the day when she can give her priceless gifts to the man of her choice. Is it too much for her to demand that she receive an equal return?' (We are, note, back into the language of commerce.) 'Going astray, it is his mother's sex that a man dishonours and drags in the dust.' Manliness had surprising stamina as reasons went. As late as 1952 Geldenhuys says of sex outside marriage: 'Every young man ought to realize that it is not only wrong, but humiliating and unmanly. Every girl should be treated as though she were your sister.'

All this is, of course, addressed to men ('it is up to you to be master of yourself,' chides Baden-Powell), and implicit in it is the essential goodness and purity of women (we are not talking about prostitutes, though many authors do). Such double standards as are assumed are not that men should go off and sow wild oats while expecting their future brides to remain chaste, but that men would naturally feel the urge to wild oats while women naturally wouldn't. Emma Drake in 1901 positively condemns those 'moral lepers' amongst men who are inclined oatwards, whose 'prevalence is alarming in the extreme'. But even when the layers of hypocrisy are later peeled back there is still no excuse to indulge. William Sadler in 1953 tells women: 'regardless of the hypocrisy of society the young woman must consider her reputation.' Succumbing to sex was the road to ruin: 'Eventually her lover will leave her for new playmates, and then she suffers from neglect, frustration, jealousy and sometimes even despair . . . Although many a young man will play around with a woman of careless virtue, he doesn't choose her for a wife but turns instead to some young woman who has kept herself free from illicit sex relations. A young fellow may profess indifference to these matters, but when it comes to marrying, as did his father and grandfathers before him, he chooses the love and devotion of a woman who has not been the sexual plaything of another man.' Geldenhuys is less sexist, but just as direct in once again resorting to financial metaphor: 'People who allow liberties to be taken with their bodies are known by the opposite sex as "cheap" and they are treated as such.'

The Third Reason for not playing around before marriage touched on the fundamental question of what sex was for in the first place. Those who thought it for reproduction and reproduction alone naturally ruled it out except within marriage – and even then under controlled circumstances. 'The very fact that conception may result at any time', writes Emma Drake, 'proves that the conjugal relation was not instituted primarily for the gratification of the lower nature, but for procreation . . . Every young person should be taught before marriage, that the closest conjugal relation should never be allowed without a willingness on the part of both that parenthood should follow.'

The Fourth Reason rolled duty to one's God, one's Country and one's race all into one. (Some managed even to bundle in medicine too, as in Dr Ernest Claxton, assistant secretary of the BMA, in 1963: 'As a doctor I can tell you that extra- and pre-marital intercourse is medically dangerous, morally degrading and nationally destructive.')

It really was a fundamental mistake, the message was drummed home, to regard sex as a matter of individual choice. Nothing could be further from the truth than to imagine that 'the question of whether or not to have sex comes down to what you think in your own mind', as Jane Cousins was to put it in 1978. More fundamental duties and responsibilities rendered what you thought in your own mind of very little consequence. 'Engaged couples', says Geldenhuys in 1952, 'should bear in mind that they have no *licence* (my italics) to perform the sex act before marriage.' In the same year Sadler seeks to impress upon men that 'they are biological torchbearers of the race' and urges them 'to keep themselves clean and healthy, worthy vehicles for the transmission of the living germ plasm from this generation to the next'. This was a throwback to earlier eugenic ancestors of thirty and more years previously, such as Charles Thompson in 1917: 'There is no man-made law to check us in the following of our impulses, but there is a race-demand that we shall check ourselves. It needs education, the constant teaching by Prophets of Fitness, to make us realize our duty as trustees of the race.' The Reverend B. W. Allen tells young men in 1919 it is man's duty to both his country and his future wife to keep himself clean: 'When temptation comes, as come it will to all, find strength in this: "I cannot give way, I cannot give way: I am a son of a King – of God." ' Baden-Powell chips in: 'Save yourself and Help to preserve the Race.'

The final sanction was that, whatever one got up to, an unseen hand was recording every dot and comma of it. Or, as the Reverend Gibson puts it so fully and chillingly in 1919: 'Though Nature never writes with a scratching pen, and though you cannot hear the record that she is making, she nevertheless writes in indelible ink and in capital letters . . . in the fibre and fabric of a man's body, in the delicate embroidery that we call our nervous system, and in his mind, memory, and will, the whole story of the crime that he commits against her when he breaks her law of chastity.' With that kind of data-base in existence, it took a strong nerve to plough on regardless.

Not for a long time did writers tackle the more pragmatic question that suggested itself: was pre-marital sex not some use in determining whether one was likely to be sexually compatible with one's future spouse? Sadler toys with the notion in 1952 before squashing it, enlisting as he descends 'a study of happiness of married couples'. This study, says Sadler, 'indicates that those who indulge in such relations are definitely sacrificing some of their chances for tranquility and happiness after marriage'. The research – dating from the 1920s and 1930s by G. V. Hamilton and Lewis Terman – proves to Sadler's satisfaction 'that pre-marital experience contributes directly to the lessening of married-life happiness'. Another unsourced 'study' quoted turns up only 10 per cent of married women who felt pre-marital sex helpful, while 80 per cent thought it 'a hindrance to early married life'. Sadler concedes that continence before marriage was neither 'the most efficient nor the most healthful state of existence'. On the other hand the worst ill-effects tended to be neurosis in people who were already unstable – not actual insanity. Women should bear in mind 'the unspeakable regret, inexpressible remorse and feeling of guilt and shame . . . the effect of engaging in these relations in parked automobiles, wayside cabins and cheap hotels is debasing and cheapening.'

Twenty years earlier in 1932 Dr M. J. Exner is more generous in conceding that 'there is no question that in some cases experience in sex relations has been of service in working out a successful relationship after marriage', just as, in 1941, Chesser thinks that 'for some individuals, a good case [can] be made out for pre-marital intercourse . . . there are some people who would feel that they cannot really make a choice of mate without prior sexual experience.' But neither of them thinks it a serious proposition for most couples. In Chesser's case this is because 'for the majority of people the very idea of pre-marital intercourse is distasteful . . . Convention is still a powerful force and not one to be disregarded. Anything which tends to lower one's personal feeling of self-respect must be ruled out . . . Nor can we afford to transgress society's code and conventions.' Exner is more concerned about the sort of women involved in such liaisons and thinks men might pick up crude and selfish mannerisms which could 'freeze women into frigidity' were they to be carried on into married life. It was little better with partners one seriously intended to marry. 'For the most part such relations are self-seeking and self-regarding only in lesser degree.' Besides which, one should consider what would happen should the engagement be called off. 'Once a woman has been fully aroused and has experienced the culmination of the sex relation, she can never be the same woman again. If her marriage does not follow, her problem now approaches that of the man.' In any event, says Exner, restraint during engagement 'may prove richly rewarding in marriage'. One didn't have to go 'all the way' to prove compatibility: 'the assurance of physical response comes long before the deeper areas are reached.'

Dr Lucia Radl in 1953 is even less keen: 'Sexual relations before marriage will not determine whether or not you and your future mate are "sexually compatible",' she writes, 'You won't learn anything of consequence and you may seriously mar or disrupt a potentially sound and happy marriage.' Dr Gilbert Oakley, ten years later, seems more worried that pre-marital sex will be incomparably more exciting than anything that is likely to occur after the wedding day – and is therefore wrong. 'Before marriage, sex is not coloured by responsibility, overshadowed by housing problems, influenced by in-laws, controlled by possibilities of child-birth. Sexual union therefore is merely an expression of the romantic moment, the glamour-ridden heavenly hours before parting cools their passion.'

A small prize for the most imaginative metaphor used to discourage creative experimentation must go to Walter Trobish, author of *I Loved a Girl*, as quoted by the Reverend O. Burrell: 'If you want to try out a parachute, you will be tempted perhaps to jump down from the top of a house or high tree. But a distance of 30 or 40 feet is not enough . . . therefore you may very well break your neck. You have to jump out of an aeroplane six thousand feet up . . . The same is true of love. You cannot try it outside of the "high flight" of marriage. Only then can its wonder really "unfold". Only then do the sex organs function as they are meant to function.' Unleashed by the rip-cord of respectability, as it were.

Those who frown on going all the way before marriage vary in how far down the track they are happy to see their readers wander. Sperry (1901) advises fiancées to monitor their loved-ones' habits closely during engagement since those who behave rather over-enthusiastically 'will be likely to commit excesses and develop perversions after marriage'. He sets narrow limits for allowable behaviour: 'She should never allow him to embrace and kiss her or fondly hold and press her hand or toy with any portion of her body. She should not permit herself to sit on his lap or nestle against him in the seductive hammock, the convenient carriage or on the tempting sofa.'

Leslie Weatherhead in 1931 is also against more or less any bodily contact during engagement since the caressing of a woman often awakens 'a sexual passion so uncontrollable that it frequently leads to self-abuse on the part of the woman, even if it does not lead to something worse'. Is there anything worse? If so, he cannot bring himself to elaborate. Unusually, Weatherhead is equally tough on both men and women: promiscuous petting is, he thinks, close to prostitution, and he quotes a colleague approvingly by way of support: 'he who uses a woman to satisfy his own sensual desires, regardless of her worth or welfare, prostitutes that woman whether with or without her consent, with or without pay.' Similarly, a woman should not 'rouse the fires of passion which a young man cannot control, which you cannot control, and which the tears of that man's mother will not be able to quench.' Sadler (1952) breaks bodily contact up into three activities. He thinks kissing permissible. Necking, he is not so sure about – 'increasingly questionable', he says. 'Deep petting' is 'still more questionable', but he is prepared to allow that 'moderate petting' is of 'definite value in preventing pre-marital sex'.

The debate is still raging twenty, even thirty, years later – though almost exclusively amongst the Christian writers. Tim and Beverly LaHaye are dead against petting, which they deal with in a section given over to some of the tricky theological questions thrown up by sex ('Is it any greater sin to have a vasectomy than to use gel contraceptives? . . . Is it right for a Christian woman to have silicone injected into her breasts? . . . How much sex or possible lust should be allowed to fill one's daily thinking?' Answers: Probably not; no; none.) As for petting? 'The price of petting should always be a marriage licence . . . because it is really "foreplay" it must be reserved for marriage.' And, for goodness' sake, oral sex? 'It's much too intimate for unmarried people. Until they are pronounced husband and wife they have no business handling each other's genitalia.' Lewis Smedes, a professor of theology, takes a more complicated view of the subject. ' "Light petting" could be wrong for some couples,' he thinks; ' "heavy petting" could be right for others.' He does, it should be said, elaborate: 'Young persons who come to petting with a solid sense of their own worth are in pretty good shape to be responsible in petting . . . persons whose initial anxiety is not balanced by a basic self-esteem are going to be very tempted to turn petting into a compulsive lunge towards the acceptance and self-love they lack.'

So how best to get through this tortuous period of courtship and engagement and the troubling, unquenchable urges it stirred up? The trouble was that it could last so long while one saved enough money to be able to wed (hence the prevalence of spermatorrhoea in young professionals who could not afford to marry during their badly-paid apprenticeships). 'Yes, lads,' sympathizes the Reverend B. W. Allen in 1919, 'it is a difficult thing to lead a clean life when the blood of youth is burning hotly in your veins.' He condemns as utterly wrong 'the social system that hinders early marriage'. His colleague the Reverend Gibson cheers his men up by indicating that St Paul was also plagued by the same feeling in his veins: 'He was a man with hot passions, whose body gave him a great deal of trouble . . . I have seen men go wrong at sixteen, and I have seen men go wrong at sixty. I do not believe that any man is safe until he is dead.' Allen advises men to steer clear of filthy conversations, foul pictures, impure books and suggestive plays. 'Join in every manly sport, in all good games; sing clean songs, read clean books.'

Avid readers of such works could, in time, build up a handy checklist of things that would only make the situation worse. A good start was to avoid unclean thoughts, especially dirty jokes. The Reverend Gibson gives the following tips for dealing with the smutty jokester: 'Take him kindly but firmly by the scruff of the neck and any part of his anatomy convenient and put him outside the billet or hut until he recollects that he is in the presence of a gentleman and British soldier, for these terms should be synonymous . . . Such a man is not funny: he is merely filthy . . . he has insulted your sister and your mother, who, when she gave you birth, walked near the edge of the grave.' Baden-Powell and Leslie Weatherhead also warn readers away from talk of 'filth', the latter appealing to 'every man and woman who reads this to agree in the name of Christ to protect others against the dirty story'.

Dancing was something else to beware of. Geldenhuys talks of the 'untold harm' caused in modern (1952) dance halls 'where too often sensual, suggestive music fills the air, where frivolity and shallowness reign and where excessive drinking takes place'. George Ryley Scott acts as agony uncle (1947) to a man of twenty-two who is similarly troubled by dancing: 'I find that dancing makes me sexually excited . . . a male friend tells me that this state will prove injurious if I don't take steps either to stop it or to find relief.' Uncle Ryley Scott offers a choice between two solutions: 'The simplest, and possibly the most satisfactory, is to get married. This may, however, for financial or other reasons, be undesirable or impossible. In any such circumstances it would be advisable to give up dancing altogether for a time.'

But the self-denial is only just beginning. Gibson advises giving up luxurious foods and over-eating as well as lying in bed in the morning ('God Bless "Reveille!" ') and adds: 'Any doctor will tell you that if you want to keep pure you must keep sober.' He recommends fresh air, exercise and washing in cold water ('it subdues his flesh and makes a man feel master of himself'). Ditto Baden-Powell ('keep the racial organ cleaned daily'), though Sadler thinks that exercise and hard mental work may actually increase 'the craving' unless carried out 'almost to the point of nervous exhaustion'. Geldenhuys adds impure thoughts and tobacco – especially in women – to the prescribed list. The Reverend Burrell warns: 'Do not spend prolonged periods of time together alone, especially at night.' Tim and Beverly LaHaye plug the Church: 'Date only Christians, for dating is the prelude to marriage.' Baden-Powell plugs the Rovers: 'You will find lots to do in the way of hiking and enjoyment of the out-of-doors and manly activities.' Especially on Sundays, for 'Sunday is the worst day in the week for vice.' Geldenhuys (1952) is also in favour of keeping busy: 'Discuss subjects of common interest, accompany each other to meetings and Church service and play games together. Lounging about in idleness should be avoided.'

Pre-marital sex is finally liberated from the quacks and the preachers – well, when? Sometime in the 1960s, certainly – you can never pin these things, Larkin-like, down to a specific year. In 1969 (1971 in the UK) Dr Eleanor Hamilton, an American psychotherapist, brought out *Sex Before Marriage*, whose very title was a defiant yah boo to her predecessors. The text sets out to dismantle a great expanse of previous prejudices in a tone every bit as confident as the one that espoused them in the first place. 'Too often', she writes, 'adults mistakenly believe in the equations:

Sexuality = intercourse
premarital intercourse = promiscuity

Both are wrong, and belief in them can lead only to repressive attitudes which, in turn, create sick sexuality.'

Or again: 'One very faulty notion that people in the past had was that young adults could walk into marriage sexually mature, with no practice and no skill, and then become sexual artists simply though a bungling sort of experimentation or by reading a book or two. Their ignorance masqueraded as "innocence" or "purity", but it was ignorance just the same, and if you look around you at the divorce statistics and then note that sex ignorance is one of the important causes for those statistics, you will know that this idea is erroneous indeed.'

Like her colleagues in the field Dr Hamilton is also concerned how far her readers ought to go; the difference being that her concern is that they won't go far enough. 'Many times young people make the mistake of *arousing* each other sexually through petting, but *not satisfying* each other. This can lead at times to negative tension . . . All in all, petting *without* orgastic release is bad business. If two teenagers do decide to pet, they would be wise to see to it that each comes to orgasm.' As for intercourse itself, Dr Hamilton lays down four conditions that any young couple should strive to meet:

(a) That they will not conceive an unwanted child.
(b) That, should they fail in their use of birth control methods, they will be able to handle the problem of an unplanned pregnancy.
(c) That they can provide an aesthetically satisfying environment for the flowering of their sexual love, such as a safe place for lovemaking without fear of interruptions or police intervention.
(d) They must be free from feelings of guilt. In other words, they must be able to tell themselves, with conviction, that what they are doing is in accord with what they believe to be right; otherwise, the sexual experience itself can be overshadowed by their fears.

These are advanced views, even for the tail-end of a decade which, as Dr Oakley tells us, kissed goodbye to the 'X' in sex. Other writers, while going along with Dr Hamilton's general line, feel obliged to throw in a reminder that there are still those who would wish the 'X' reinstated in 72 point Gothic Bold. 'There is one disadvantage that ought to be mentioned,' Wardell B. Pomeroy warns girls in the same year. 'It is the fact that society has a certain amount of disapproval of petting, and as a result of this, it is possible that the girl's reputation may be damaged.' But in his list of pros and cons Pomeroy seems to come down on the side of the value of a trial run with a future husband: 'it is a good way for her to find out if she's going to enjoy the constant intimacy of the bedroom with that particular young man.' By the mid-1970s the debate is exhausted for the more liberal-minded writers. The *SAR Guide* in 1975 dismisses the question with a rhetorical shrug: 'If sex is prohibited before marriage, how can you be expected to perform perfectly after you get married?' For perfect performance should by now be everyone's goal, not to mention everyone's right. 'Remember', the guide adds, 'there is no right way or wrong way to express your sexuality, only your way.'

Not that moral debate vanishes altogether. 'J' has her own pokerwork five-point set of ethical guidelines for the sensuous woman which runs as follows: '1. I believe a woman must keep her hands off her sister's and best friend's man. 2. I believe it is immoral for a woman to let a man she doesn't like touch her – even if that man is her husband. 3. I believe it is immoral for a woman not to give herself completely to a man she loves. 4. I believe it is moral for a woman to give herself to a man she respects, likes and is sexually attracted to, as long as she doesn't betray a promise of fidelity she has made to another man. 5. I believe a woman has a moral obligation not to tease, lead on or in other ways emotionally and physically torture a man whose love and sexuality she cannot return.'

Even the most free and alternative spirits continue to ask themselves how far they should go. Helen Gurley Brown can't quite decide: 'Sleeping with more than one man on the same day or in the same week could be considered promiscuous, I suppose, yet I think you can do quite a lot of that and *not* be promiscuous . . . Now, you can't have sex with *everyone* who asks you or attracts you . . . you'd just get too frazzled, and also, sex would lose its *meaning*. Nevertheless, I think you can be multifriended.' Dr Alex Comfort manages to distil all ethical concerns down to a more manageable formula. He maintains that there are just two main 'rules' in good sex. One is 'don't do anything you don't really enjoy' and the other is 'find your partner's needs and don't balk them if you can help it.' As for those who disagree? Dr Comfort thinks it safe to say that anyone who suggests that something two people enjoy doing together might be immature or unhealthy is probably talking tosh.

Hereafter books seek to outbid one other to be the most 'non-judgemental'. *The Complete Book of Love and Sex* (1983) claims to be the ultimate in such works by assuring readers it is 'totally non-judgemental . . . we don't condemn anyone for what they are or what they do'. The authors offer a step-by-step guide to adolescent sex, much in the manner of a non-judgemental colour supplement cookery course. There are tips on dating and kissing ('make it brief and sexless, but on the lips' . . . 'slobbering noises and wet kisses are usually unacceptable and should be avoided' . . . 'you will become pleasantly aroused and may confuse this with being in love . . . try not to say "I love you" in the first flush of excitement'). The results of the authors' survey on what people like during petting follows ('Twice as many men squeezed their partners' breasts as wanted it done'), together with further handy hints ('All breast play is best done with the girl's bra undone or it is uncomfortable').

When the first two Kinsey reports appeared in the late forties and early fifties they revealed a volume of pre-marital sexual activity that could never have been guessed at from reading contemporary sex or marriage manuals. The non-judgemental school of authorship seeks to narrow the divide between what happens and what the writer thinks should happen. Thus Pomeroy, in discussing petting, accepts that 'almost without exception girls pet before marriage, at some time or other, and petting to orgasm is more common with the new generation.' Likewise, *The Complete Book of Love and Sex* states calmly: 'Whilst accepting that some couples do not have intercourse during courtship, the majority do, and this must now be accepted as the norm, whatever one's individual moral views on the subject.' Indeed, the authors warn against the man who 'professes no healthy sexual desire for his beloved and will not have intercourse with her "because he respects her" '. Such a man, they advise, is not always what he seems. 'Clinical experience shows that that very often such males are unhappy about sex and their new brides frequently come for help some months later complaining that he still "respects" her.' Poor man. Maybe he is simply working from a secondhand sex manual and is (a) frightened of undermining his nervous system; (b) anxious about contracting syphilis; (c) worried what Nature's scratching pen will engrave on his file card.

Alternatively, he may just be a former Rover.

5

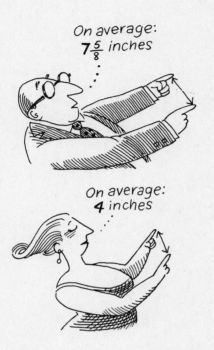

Breeding: Birds and Bees

We stand now on the threshold of marriage and it will shortly do no harm to learn a little biology. But first let us be sure we are marrying the right person. There is, for instance, the question of age. Authorities differ on this, so the best we can do is to quote a sample of opinions on the subject. Mrs A. M. Longshore-Potts in 1895 states unequivocally that twenty-five is the proper age for a man to marry and that his bride should be twenty-one. Sperry in 1900 thinks the best results follow from marriages when the man is between twenty-two and twenty-eight and the woman between twenty and twenty-five. Van de Velde in 1926 advises the man to wait until he is thirty and the woman between twenty-three and twenty-five.

If we are wise we will be marrying a Christian for, as Tim and Beverly LaHaye demonstrate in 1976, Christians have better sex lives than non-Christians. You demand their evidence? They begin with a survey of 100,000 women in *Redbook* magazine which showed that 'with notable consistency, the greater the intensity of a woman's religious convictions, the likelier she is to be highly satisfied with the sexual pleasures of marriage . . . strongly religious women seem to be more responsive and . . . more likely than non-religious women to be orgasmic every time [they] engage in sex.' The specifically Christian dimension comes from Tim himself. 'Years of counselling predominantly Christian couples have convinced me that Christian men and women experience a higher degree of orgasmic enjoyment than non-Christians.' But we need not simply take Tim's word for it since he is able to quote from the research of a Dr Herbert J. Miles. From a sample of 151 Christian couples Dr Miles found that 96.1 per cent of wives had experienced 'a definite orgasm', which, Tim says, is 'a remarkable improvement over the secular norm'. He adds: 'It is safe to say that, except for Christians, the majority of women do not regularly enjoy orgasm in the act of marriage. In fact, many don't even know what it is.'

So, yes, let's be sure to marry a Christian. (Though those of us who are Rovers at heart may wish to take Baden-Powell's advice and marry a girl-guide: 'You get wives in this way who can be better pals because they have got the same keenness on camping and the out-of-doors with all the . . . handiness . . . health and good temper that comes of such life'.) The men amongst us might even offer up a little eve-of-marriage prayer suggested by Geldenhuys in 1952: 'I will be tenderly loving and considerate to my Beloved. Although God's Word teaches that the man is the head of the house, I will bear in mind that this does not mean that I may rule over her with a heavy hand . . . I cannot demand intercourse with my Beloved when she is tired or unresponsive . . . I should take an interest in her work, clothes, personal appearance. I must as frequently as possible arrange some recreation for her; take her for an outing or to hear some good music or provide some other form of healthy recreation. As regards our home, I must provide it with the necessary furniture and other requirements as far as our means allow. I must bring her a bunch of flowers occasionally.'

If we are readers of Gavin Reid, author of *Starting Out Together* (1981) we will, at this stage, be frank with each other about any previous sexual experience, for 'to discover this later, after marriage, can often deeply hurt the husband or wife'. We may also consider each having a physical examination and perhaps also asking the doctor for a certificate of clean health. Van de Velde 'emphatically supports' the notion of standardized medical inspection and certification before marriage while Dr Emma Drake suggests in 1901 that one's doctor may be able to offer further guidance: 'in discovering the character of your daughter's associates the family physician should be a valuable assistant. If he be a friend as well as physician, he will gladly come to your aid.' For their part men should be wary of marrying 'beneath them'. Dr Rennie MacAndrew (1928) has a sensible word of advice here: 'Men should grasp the fact that there is the same type of girl in every stratum of society.' Another commonsense tip from Dr MacAndrew is to go for a swim with her/him before committing oneself too deeply: 'mixed bathing now is a great aid to judge how the sight of another's body is likely to affect one.'

Regrettably, but it must be said, there are some who should not be thinking of marriage at all. Sperry lists the categories: 'Many

weaklings, invalids and defectives, both physical and mental . . .
both for their own good and for the good of mankind, ought never
to marry at all.' This is quite apart from the 'insane, lepers,
epileptics and syphilitics' who, Dr Sperry supposes, we would all
readily agree should not be allowed up the aisle.

But Dr Sperry himself would go further: 'It is almost equally
evident that persons who are decidedly scrofulous, consumptive or
cancerous should not intermarry; and it is questionable whether
persons of such morbid tendency ought ever to marry at all.' One
should not simply consider one's own background. Cast the mind
around one's relatives, as well: 'Those who spring from families in
which monomania, dipsomania, kleptomania, etc. are common,
are in great danger of helping to perpetuate defects of which the
world sorely needs to be relieved . . . there are many who ought,
practically, to conduct themselves as if they were eunuchs, for the
sake of humanity.' Those who are especially tall, short, fat, lean or
indolent, need not necessarily contemplate the harem but should
avoid marrying someone of their own size or disposition. 'Fortunately nature usually inclines people to see their opposites for
associates in marriage.'

But fatties, kleptoes, drunks and epileptics need not be
despondent. Charles Thompson (1917), another rigorous eugenic
thinker, hastens to assure us that he does not advocate the 'lethal
chamber'. It is simply that, if one does not fall into the 'wholesome
scheme of things' one does not have a right to propagate. He
himself would rule out the 'feeble-minded, cretins, deaf mutes,
insanes, dipsomaniacs and epileptics, the idiots, and probably the
consumptives'. Again, one's GP may be able to help: 'A man
should not be averse to taking his doctor's opinion upon the
desirability of his marrying.'

One only has to look at the statistics produced in the House of
Lords in 1926 – quoted by Edward Griffiths in 1941 – for the
breakdown of births per 1,000 married people under the age of
fifty:

Schoolmasters 93
Clergy.. 102
Doctors and professional men 103
Skilled labourers 153
Unskilled labourers 247

Throw in the fact that 10 per cent of the population is insane, epileptic, paupers, criminal, mentally deficient and so on – two-thirds of whom can breed 'quite indiscriminately' – and one begins to see what the eugenisists are driving at. Thompson is able to offer some comfort: 'Fortunately – it sounds a hard saying, but eminent sociologists have expressed the view – the death-rate corresponds closely to the birth-rate . . . Bad housing, low wages, and consequent poor nutrition – these are the disabilities under which the poor labour; and so their children die like flies.' There is always a silver lining.

Both Marie Stopes and 'A Physician' go along with some form of sterilization programme for those unfit to breed. Dr Stopes recommends sterilization by X-rays as the most humane method. But by the 1950s the list of disqualifying afflictions is dwindling. Dr Hutton in 1953 mentions only unspecified genetic disorders and advises women epileptics in particular never to think of marrying.

But for those who do not fall into any of the above categories, it is time to acquire a knowledge of the basic equipment of marriage. The first question to get out of the way is the matter of size and whether or not it matters. We speak, inevitably, of white American or British male organs, for as Dr van de Velde reminds us in 1926, the question of size is racially-determined: 'Negroes, for example, are generally longer and more massive, than white men; and they also number among them, proportionally to their own large average, more extreme "phallic giants" than the whites.' Van de Velde also thinks genitals smell differently from race to race.

There are statistics which may be of some help in putting male readers' minds at rest. In flaccid state the average length is between $2\frac{5}{8}$ and $4\frac{5}{8}$ inches (Exner); or anything between 2 and 8 inches (LaHaye); or about 2 or 3 inches (Cousins). Erect, it is between 4 and $7\frac{1}{2}$ inches (Exner); or about 6 inches (van de Velde, Comfort and Cousins); or 6 to 8 (LaHaye). There are no short cuts to such personal knowledge. 'It is hardly possible to draw any correct inference', says van de Velde, 'from the general bodily build and stature of a man . . . as to the size of phallus.' Unless he's a negro, of course.

Does size matter? Exner thinks not: 'Size has but little to do with the ability to satisfy the beloved.' LaHaye goes further: 'In all probability no man has ever really been too small', while Comfort considers that 'functionally' size is wholly unimportant. But then all these verdicts come from men. Jane Cousins is notably more guarded in voicing her opinion that 'the size of a penis *need* [my italics] make no difference to anyone's sexual pleasure.' 'Size isn't supposed to matter, any more than a woman's breast size matters,' writes Helen Gurley Brown. 'Well, you know perfectly well breast size *matters* – they just say that to cheer up us small-chested ones – and there is nothing like a *big* . . . longing-to-be-appreciated . . . lovely male penis to bring tears to the eyes and joy to the psyche.' On the other hand Ms Gurley Brown includes in this oration 'anything over 4 inches erect', which almost falls off the bottom end of the above scale. She adds: 'These are admiring things to *say* to a man: "This is the most beautiful one in the world . . . This is the *biggest* one in the world." ' 'J' advocates a more cautious approach: 'Don't lie. If he has a small penis and you tell him it's the biggest one in the world, he's not going to believe you.' Van de Velde sides with the women: 'On the whole, a phallus of unusual size must be more agreeable to women, on account of increased pressure and friction in coitus.' Though the organ's visual appeal is evidently quite lost on him: 'the membrum virile is far from aesthetically attractive; in fact, so little lovely that painters and sculptors habitually represent it as smaller and more insignificant than it really is.'

Harvey Gochros and Joel Fisher, in urging readers to *Treat Yourself to a Better Sex Life* (1980), add a touch of gruesome realism to the matter of obsession with size: 'The adolescent learns early that the most important, central item in playing the all-important sexual game well is a major-league penis. Without a top-notch penis he feels relegated to the bush league. How does the growing sexual athlete learn to evaluate his athletic equipment? He has plenty of opportunities. He checks out his teammates' equipment in the locker room, showers and at the urinals; he listens to countless dirty stories told by his teammates . . . based on these observations he concludes that a good penis has to be awe-inspiring in size and hard as steel.'

Gochros and Fisher ask men calmly to accept that there are organs and organs. 'These differences can be important. They can certainly affect a man's self-image, and fear of revealing a relatively small penis to a potential partner has kept many a man from seeking sexual partners. And there are women who do prefer big penises; there are even some women who downright insist upon them . . . On the other hand there are many women who couldn't care less or who hardly even notice the size of their partner's penis. Indeed, some women are physically uncomfortable with big penises.'

Less time is spent on reassuring women, and more on precise anatomical exploration of their muscular structures, together with involved recitations of their Latin tags. Van de Velde identifies the *sphincter vaginae, constrictor cunni, musculus levator vaginae*, the *bulbi vestibuli*, the *portio vaginalis uteri*, the *fornix vaginae*, the *fornix anterior, laguear anerius*, the *ligamenta rotunda*, the *ligamenta lata*, together with instructions on their development and control. Later writers concentrate on the pubococcygeous muscles – PCs for short – and the PC-improving Kegel exercises, originally intended for solving urinary incontinence, but now harnessed in the universal pursuit of the five-star orgasm. ('Do these exercises AT LEAST ONCE PER DAY FOR THE REMAINDER OF THE GROWTH PROGRAMME' – Heiman and Lopiccolo.)

Reliance is generally placed on the diagrammatic arts – and, more recently, photography – to put readers in the picture as to women's physiology. Written descriptions of the female organs are not always successful. Dr Marion Greaves, in an appendix to Weatherhead's book in 1931, hazards a genteel image to convey the clitoris – 'like the stump-end of a whist-card pencil'. Exner is more adventurous with the vagina: 'In elasticity it might be compared to a rubber glove which can fit the hand of a Japanese girl or a charwoman . . . to the touch it resembles the inside of an orange if one imagines that fruit to be composed of small muscles and tissues.' The 'G-Spot' makes a late and vague appearance after a prominent marketing operation in 1982 – some thirty years after 'G' (Graffenburg, Ernst) had more modestly covered the ground in an obscure Bombay-published journal of sexology.

That this form of instruction was necessary is not doubted by most writers. Marie Stopes was, she said, largely motivated to write *Married Love* by the 'terrible price of sex-ignorance' she herself paid during her own first marriage (though it was written before meeting her second husband, Humphrey Verdon Roe). Similarly, van de Velde states his belief that 'most married people do not know the ABC of sex', though he addresses his teaching to men 'for they are naturally educators and initiators of their wives in sexual matters'. And yet 'the average husband does not know that there are numberless delicate differentiations and modifications of sexual pleasure, all lying strictly within the bounds of normality which can banish the mechanical monotony . . . He thinks his wife is "far above that sort of thing", leaves her more and more to herself, seeks the diversity of stimulation he needs outside his home, and often ends in real debauchery in consequence.' The matching ignorance of women is set out in 1897 by Ellis Ethelmer: 'Frequently, and shamefully, woman is left to enter upon marriage without true knowledge or any warning as to the real nature of the wife's so-called "duties" therein; its possible physical relations of perhaps the most repugnant or even perilous character to herself – abuses and excesses resultant often in misery, suffering or premature death, but which she finds to be assumed as part of the "iron contract".'

There is just one other thing to sort out before forging the iron contract, and that is whether one's intended shares one's view towards children. To Sperry's way of thinking, there is no doubt as to how one's intended should respond. A case of someone wanting even to delay the tiny patter 'generally means that they want to enjoy the pleasures of *lust* for a season'. Without children, he argues, thoughts turn to 'dissipation and extravagance. Perhaps their lustful activities, growing restless under legal restraint, break out as immoral and illegal intrigues and liaisons which increase till elopement, suicide or murder turn their farce of marriage into an awful tragedy.' By contrast, 'the raising of children tends decidedly to the healthfulness of parents by preventing the sexual excesses, unnatural practices, which are so apt to creep into childless families. Much of the married life of many childless couples is practically given up to sex gluttony, and is but little short of legalized prostitution.' Emma Drake agrees in 1901: 'That many marriages are little better than licensed prostitution seems a hard thing to say, but when the lower nature is petted and indulged in at the expense of the higher, it is a just thing to say, however harsh it may seem.'

But then the barricades against birth control begin to tumble and by 1909 Pastor Ernest Bars (quoted by van de Velde) is conceding that 'the desire for parentage has receded into the background, compared to the desire for sexual relations.' But don't rule it out altogether. Oakley, in 1963, thinks that, for spiritual reasons, couples should be prepared to have at least one child. The

Reverend Barry Chant chimes in with characteristic antipodean directness. Sex without trying to conceive, he says is like 'wanting only dessert without any vegetables'. Barry explains: 'Like eating vegetables, raising children has its moments of unpleasantness, but in the long run it is satisfying and enjoyable.'

But there are those, of course, who have never gone for the puritan appeal of greens and remain addicted to puddings. Enter 'Recreational Sex' – Marketing Director: Dr Alex Comfort. 'The best modern sex', he announces in 1973, 'is nonreproductive.' An enjoyable erotic life, he pronounces, must have privacy – the sort of privacy you don't get with children in the house. That is *More Joy of Sex*. Plain old *Joy* advises : 'the sort of sex we . . . are talking about here almost excludes fertility' – couples who aren't prepared to make sacrifices should stick to having sex and not have children.

The important thing, say Gochros and Fisher, is for you, and you alone to decide. If you want their point of view, it is that 'love, sex and commitment are three separate and different human experiences, and that many of our problems comes from blurring the differences among the three. Each can exist without the other two. Each may enhance and each may detract from one or both of the others.' Moreover, they think that increasing numbers of men and women agree. 'Purely recreational sex is not only all right for them, but may be preferred.' But once again, as judges are so fond of telling their juries, it is entirely a matter for you to decide.

6

How Often? How Long? How?

From now on very little is up to you. There is an authoritarian streak in most writers of sex manuals which is going to unleash itself now you are married. They want you learning the right habits early. Start off as they mean you to continue.

So the first thing to consider is frequency and we will begin in 1901 with Lyman B. Sperry, who has set views on this, as with many other matters. 'It may be safe to state', he states, 'that the ordinary man can safely indulge about four times a month.' Subject, of course, to his wife's condition and wishes. 'More than that would be excess for, perhaps, a large majority of civilized men and women.'

Within these bounds – and provided the activity is 'naturally conducted' – Sperry thinks that sex may even prove beneficial. But this assumes that conjugal gratification will only occur when there exists surplus energy (or, 'vigor flowing at high tide') and, even then, within strict confines. 'People should never indulge when they really doubt the wisdom of it. Sexual excitement should not be indulged when either party is consciously fatigued in body or mind; nor should it be allowed to immediately precede severe effort of body or mind. Indulgence should also be avoided just before and after eating or bathing. Sexual activity exhausts vitality; hence, when one is fatigued, worried, digesting food or reacting from a bath, the vital energies are deeply engaged in important business. At such times vitality says to sexual desire: "I am otherwise engaged." '

Once a week is a little on the severe side, even for 1900. Jules Guyot's 1857 book of advice for Prince Napoleon, reissued in the 1930s, was rather more interested in what desire had to say than in vitality's prim excuses. He thought that most women would feel a need for union once every three days. Marie Stopes quotes Luther's advice – 'two or three connections a week in marriage, at the highest sexual power' – which was still being wheeled out in the 1950s.

But Stopes tends to a more complicated view of desire than Luther – and of women's desire in particular, for it was this that counted for most. 'If the wife has, as I think the majority of healthy, well-fed young women will be found to have, a fortnightly conscious or unconscious *potentiality* of desire, then the two should find a perfect mutual adjustment in having fortnightly unions.' But masculine desire was not to be wholly disregarded, for 'many men, who can well practise restraint for 12 or 14 days, will find that one union only will not then thoroughly satisfy them.' Ditto healthy women. The answer was a modest binge every two weeks. 'Have three or four days of repeated unions, followed by about 10 days without any unions at all, unless some strong external stimulus has stirred a mutual desire.' She suggests that a picture, novel, anniversary or poem might act in such a way.

But Mrs Stopes is alive to the possibility of variation in libido. What, she asks, should a strongly-sexed husband do if married to a wife who only desired union once a month? Restrain himself 'at any cost' for two weeks and then 'set himself ardently to woo her', when he would be most likely to succeed. 'A fortnight', she thinks, 'is not too long for a healthy man to restrain himself with advantage.' In support of her view she cites Sir Thomas Clouston's *Before I Wed* (1913): 'Nature has so arranged matters that the more constantly control is exercised the more easy and effective it becomes. It becomes a habit. The less control is exercised the greater tendency there is for a desire to become a *craving* of an uncontrollable kind which is itself of the nature of disease, and means *death* sooner or later.'

Weatherhead thinks twice a week average for a 'healthy man who does little creative work'. This drops to once in ten days for 'those who unconsciously use sex energy in other ways'. Self-controlled men could get by on once or twice a month if practising the 'safe period' though Weatherhead concedes that 'this so-called "safe period" coincides with a woman's disinclination and not her desire'. Unfortunate, that.

Exner, a better feminist, advises compromise between warring libidos. Husbands, in particular, should make concessions. 'Must every erection occurring at night, for example, be made the occasion for waking the wife out of sound sleep one or more times for coitus?' The very soul of consideration, you see. MacAndrew is modesty itself in 1928: 'Once every week or 10 days would undoubtedly not be excessive for those on this side of 55, while those who are older would be entirely safe to practise it once fortnightly or monthly.' Wives with stronger sexual urges than their husbands should sublimate them as best they could – 'i.e. take up useful hobbies, especially those requiring mental effort'.

Chesser's learning goes beyond Luther to Mohammed (every eight days) and Socrates (every ten days). Himself, he merely advises moderation. 'Just as with meals and bathing one must avoid extremes yet acquire regular habits, something of the same is true of sexual life. I say only "something of the same", for anything like a regular routine, a keeping to a timetable is undesirable.' A similar moderation is urged by Geldenhuys: 'Some find once in three weeks the best. Others once in 10 days, and others more frequently.' Amazing as it may seem.

Luther crops up once again in Isabel Emslie Hutton's advice. 'For some people, however, even this may seem rather excessive . . . an average of once a week is perhaps more suitable . . . Even this average is too great for some people. Healthy, vigorous couples may indulge in more frequent intercourse but they should not exceed, as a rule, the average of two unions in each week.' Whether for moral or medical grounds she does not make entirely clear.

It is not until Gilbert Oakley that the refrain changes: 'If the act is performed several times a week in an atmosphere of harmony and mutual satisfaction the health of the individual is more likely to be maintained than injured.' Even MacAndrew agrees it is good for you – as good, say, as 'a sea bathe or a game of tennis'. He adds: 'It is for this reason that married people need less physical exercise than the single.' Even once-a-week married people.

The writers who restrain their didactic instincts over the question of frequency are rare. Van de Velde limits himself to advising husbands not to arouse expectations in their wives that they will not be able to sustain. 'We only know, and indisputably, that there are perfectly healthy and normal men in their most vigorous years who can only execute coitus twice a week, and at the very utmost and in exceptional circumstances, once a day – and that there are others who can repeat the act three or four or more times in succession or at very brief intervals during several days, without any injury to health and zest.' Not to mention wives (he doesn't). Alex Comfort knows of even more prodigious feats – men who can manage 'more than six full orgasms in only a few hours provided they aren't "timestressed" [sic]'. He adds felicitously: 'You can no more "have too much sex" than you can over-empty a toilet cistern.' As for too little? 'Much under twice a week suggests you could be getting more out of it.' Can you under-empty a toilet system? Never mind. It is, in any case, just the sort of talk that the *Complete Book of Love and Sex* frowns on: 'One of the greatest problems in modern marriage is that the sex books have so conditioned people to believe that everyone else is having a stunning sex life that the average couple having intercourse moderately satisfactorily a couple of times a week feel that they must be abnormally under-sexed or even no good at all.' Pause only to spare a thought for the generations led by the sex books to believe that they were abnormally over-sexed.

Now we have sorted out this question of frequency we can at last concern ourselves with the act itself. Van de Velde spends some little time defining it ('by the term sexual intercourse we herewith designate the full range of contact and connection, between human beings, for sexual consummation ... which aims, directly or indirectly, at the consummation of sexual satisfaction, and which, having achieved a certain degree of stimulation concludes with ... etc. etc.'), but we may perhaps take all this as understood. However, van de Velde's further breakdown of the composite ingredients of the act should be noted since more or less everyone subsequently faithfully adopts them in their own writings. They are, says van de Velde: 'The prelude, the love play, the sexual union; and the after-play, epilogue or after-glow (postlude).' Of these, the third stage should, he says, be called coitus, 'but I shall call it *communion*'.

We shall stay with van de Velde a while, for, having set out these definitions, he then plunges into a tidal wave of detail which sweeps the reader on for the next 100 pages – except that that suggests rather too much passion for what is actually a colossal iceberg of prose. But the iceberg is nevertheless a revelation to those who imagine foreplay to have been a contemporary of Carnaby Street or kaftans, the more so since van de Velde's definition of the act includes 'the nearly simultaneous culmination of sensation – or orgasm – of both partners'.

The prelude to van de Velde's 'love drama' is the kiss ('the prototype of all erotic contact'), which blends imperceptibly into love-play. Omitting love-play, says van de Velde, is 'unpardonably *stupid*' except on very rare occasions between practised lovers – 'between persons of finer feelings, and only such are capable of Ideal Marriage'. The *motifs* of the prelude are *coquetry* and *flirtation*. Each is defined at some length.

In all, there are nearly five pages on the prelude. Love-play occupies a further eighteen pages, beginning with an exposition of 'varieties of the *genus* kiss'. The senses involved in *bucco-lingual* kissing are explored, together with the tactile sensations of suction, the use of the teeth, the *olfactory* or *inhalation* method, the sensations received by the outer epidermis and the role and morality of the love-bite. That has seen to another ten pages, whence we progress methodically to consideration of *erogenous zones* – also imagined by today's teenagers to be one of the peripheral innovations of the first Wilson administration.

The 'high erotic value' of breasts is dissected first. 'Mammillary stimulation is agreeable to the stimulator as well as to the passive partner, but generally to a lesser degree, and in a predominantly *psychic* mode, through the consciousness of conferred pleasure.' You will by now be recalling J. Johnson Abraham's approving testimony on van de Velde's writing being 'completely without a scintilla of eroticism'. Next under the knife is 'local stimulation', with especial emphasis on 'the charm of *reciprocity*' in this area. The male reader will learn the technique of attending to the *glans clitoridis*; the female, the art of penile stimulation. The differences in male and female responses are explained. Herbal preparations and lubricants are mentioned, together with a Dover Street address at which Dr van de Velde's own brand can be obtained.

It is only in discussing oral sex that van de Velde's nerve fails him. He analyses its mechanism and effects and emphasizes 'the need for aesthetic delicacy and discretion', but thinks it 'unnecessary to describe the technique of this form of genital stimulation. It may be constructed from what has already been said in detail about the kiss in general, and about the special structure of the feminine organs.'

This omission apart, van de Velde's exposition of the first two scenes from Love Drama is so comprehensive that more or less everyone since has taken it as their starting point, and not a few as their finishing point as well. So we should just look at what others have to say on oral sex before moving on to communion itself.

MacAndrew confines himself to declaring 'body osculation' quite normal and something practised 'by wise married lovers if they so desire in all countries where sex is not looked upon as unclean'. Chesser warns against attempting it on honeymoon. Heiman and Lopiccolo and 'J' give extensive instruction ('the butterfly flick, the silken swirl, the hoover, the whipped cream wriggle' – you get the picture), while Alex Comfort devotes three pages of *The Joy of Sex* to the art of 'mouth music' ('practise on a thumb'). Helen Gurley Brown has a ten-point course of instructions ('from a friend who claims to be "the best in the world" '). 'J' tells those who are revolted by the prospect that they are 'probably a typical product of current taboos against oral gratification'.

Which is just the sort of talk Tim and Beverly LaHaye have come to expect in this day and age. Tim and Beverly cite a survey which shows oral sex to be on the increase. This, they are sure, is 'thanks to amoral sex education, pornography, modern sex literature and the moral breakdown of our times'. They add superfluously: 'Obviously the Christian community has not unanimously accepted oral sex.'

The Christian community is in some difficulty over the matter since the Bible, according to Tim and Beverly, is completely silent on the subject. 'We do not personally recommend it or advocate it, but we have no Biblical grounds for forbidding it between married people who mutually enjoy it.' Nevertheless, it was to Tim and Beverly's 'amazement' that 77 per cent of ministers surveyed felt that oral sex was acceptable. They conclude from the survey that the habit 'has in recent years been given unwarranted publicity. We are confident that nothing will ever replace the traditional act of marriage.'

Alexandra Penney strikes a middle course. It is a sure way to make your man feel he's had a 'fireworks orgasm', she says but it is 'certainly not an obligation . . . don't do anything that repels you.' Oral sex, the way she sees it, is a little like learning to swim: 'Once you've mastered the basics – and they are fairly easy – you may want to advance further and really perfect your technique. Nature is on your side.' Not to mention the media.

And so to communion itself. We have already considered its frequency. Now we must ask, where shall it take place? Marie Stopes has the firmest views on this, not out of consideration for the lovers themselves so much as out of a conviction that the circumstances of conception are of vital influence on the nature of the consequent child. 'Even in our present degraded civilization', she writes in *Radiant Motherhood*, 'there are some who do realize the sacredness and the value of nature and sunlight. There must be many beautiful children who were conceived from unions which took place under natural conditions of light and open air radiance. The most spontaneous time for conception is the summer when our air is mild and sweet enough for true love in nature's way.' But she concedes that it will 'in all probability long remain only possible for most lovers to ramble together in nature, and then later to follow the usual course of uniting within their room'.

Probability is not something Rennie MacAndrew is content should govern such things. 'Intimacy', he writes, adopting contemporary idiom, 'should always take place on top of the bed rather than beneath the blankets, so that each can enjoy seeing the physical charms of the other. Exhibitionism is not a perversion as a prologue to the consummation of love. Ideally, intercourse should be performed in a dimly lighted room, certainly not in the dark.'

Mrs Stopes apart, the great majority of writers take it as read that union will occur in or on a bed. 'A warm bedroom furnished with a firm yet resilient bed takes a lot of beating,' says the *Sun*'s *101 Questions About Sex*. Even Alex Comfort considers the bed to be the most important piece of domestic sexual equipment, though literal readers may be faced by the prospect of having to have one custom-built to Dr Comfort's specifications – the height needs to be just right, for one thing, the top of the mattress exactly level with the man's pubic bone. Then there are those who will wish to try experiments along the lines of Dr Comfort's section on bondage, in which case 'bedposts are essential'. He recommends four pillows and no electric blanket: 'The sort you lie on will in any case not stand up to sexual intercourse.' Furthermore, there will be a bedside cabinet with enough drawers to hold any 'extras' such as, for instance, a 'bataca' – a soft plastic foam bat 'with which you can belt each other at full strength without hurting'. Stools, cushions, big mirrors inside cupboard doors and a gymnastic mat are additional suggested accoutrements. Indeed, says the doctor, 'really enthusiastic sex usually involves almost every piece of furniture in the house'. A well-designed bedroom should be a 'sexual gymnasium' without being an embarrassment to any stray elderly relatives. Ever practical, Dr Comfort tells us that semen can be removed from furniture 'either with a stiff brush, when the stain has dried, or with a dilute solution of sodium bicarbonate'.

Other recent writers are less baroque, not to mention expensive, in their tastes and recommend alternative locations mainly for the sake of variety. 'For a change tonight,' Marabel Morgan urges aspiring total women, 'after the children are in bed place a lighted candle on the floor and seduce him under the dining room table. Or lead him to the sofa. How about the hammock? Or in the garden. He may say "We don't have a hammock". You can reply "Oh darling, I forgot." ' Spontaneous-like. Motels, recommended for therapeutic purposes by Masters and Johnson, feature high in American writers' locations. Heiman and Lopiccolo suggest a night out in one. Or else: 'You might try the back seat of the family car at a drive-in movie, or parked in a more discreet place, such as your own garage, if necessary. Consider the woods (watch out for poison ivy), your living room couch, the kitchen floor, or a borrowed tent in your backyard.'

If there is a place for everything, so there is a time. Rennie MacAndrew, for instance, believes there to be only one appropriate time for intimacy: 'Night is the proper time as greater benefit is gained if sleep follows.' There is also the time to be allowed. Heiman and Lopiccolo remind readers of one of the most startling findings to emerge from the 1948 Kinsey Report into male sexual behaviour; that for 75 per cent of men intercourse was over within two minutes of starting. But, doctor, what is normal? MacAndrew is characteristically dogmatic: 'From the beginning of foreplay to the end of the afterplay ought not to occupy less than quarter of an hour, probably about half an hour is the usual time. More than an hour is rather long, but each hungry erotic part should receive its quota of caresses and stimulation.' The *Sun* guide tells readers to 'think in terms of half an hour to an hour' for foreplay, which may explain why they have so little time left to read a daily paper. Isabel Hutton is more modest: 'With controlled movements some men can continue the coitus for 15 to 20 minutes, or even longer.' Chesser writes of other men who do not merely rely on controlled movements – 'men who, in order to turn their minds away from the sexual act, interrupt the proceedings in order to smoke or even eat or drink.' Chesser is not wholly in favour of such diversions. But we have ourselves interrupted the proceedings enough. It is time to consider positions.

7

Missionary

Zeal

Sex manuals are famous as gazeteers of contortion, Baedekers of gymnastics. Their reputation travels in advance, so that the pubescent schoolboy can recite snatches of the acrobatic tantra – the Crab, the Half-lotus, the Monkey, the Snake-spirit, the Knee-elbow, the Thunderbolt or the Tripod. He knows there to be at least – oooh – 350, though there is a boy in the Sixth who claims to be aware of 490.

Disillusionment is swift. He discovers that the paperback Koka Shastra in the local W. H. Smith can only manage fifty-four, and not even Nureyev would be fool enough to try half of them. And when he finally stumbles across a battered copy of *Ideal Marriage* at the PTA fête bookstall he is stunned to find a measly ten.

Nor, if he continues his researches, can he simply put this down to mere prudery or a failure of imagination on the part of the old Dutch gynaecologist. Helena Wright lists only five; Parkinson-Smith struggles to come up with seven, Hutton manages six, Gochros and Fisher and the LaHayes each vouchsafe four. The *Sun*, with all its wealth of experience, can only produce a guide containing ten. The *Encyclopaedia of Sexual Knowledge*, co-authored improbably enough by a Dr A. Willy (Arthur Koestler under a pseudonym) in 1934, contrives to produce thirteen by sub-dividing some of van de Velde's categories. Exner devotes a solitary paragraph to the subject; Jane Cousins dispatches the subject in six. And Alex Comfort? Oh, the disappointment. Dr Comfort is disdainful of the whole business: The majority of the 'non-freak' ones come naturally, he says, and 'few of the freak postures merit more than a single visit out of curiosity'.

Then there are those who consider even a single visit one too many. Sperry thinks that a study of diagrams 'will suggest the important fact that the horizontal one is the proper one for sexual union.' He observes what many authors observe; that it is only humans who face each other, an important factor, he thinks, in elevating them above animals.

That there are alternatives to the customary position Sperry is willing to concede. What he is not willing to do is rehearse them. 'It is not necessary to describe in detail the proper position for copulation or the exact methods of procedure in exercising the sexual function,' he writes, adding simply: 'It may, however, be well to say that any position that is painful to the wife should be religiously avoided.' This is echoed by George Ryley Scott in *Your Sex Questions Answered*. He warns: 'Any variation from the orthodox position may, in certain circumstances, prove dangerous.' Whereupon he proceeds to consider the disturbing question: 'Does the sex act ever cause the death of the husband or wife?'

So, let van de Velde once more be our punctilious and passionless guide to what he terms 'position and action during coitus'. Teasingly, he too hints at the 100 or more attitudes contained in certain oriental encyclopaedias, of which he will pass on only ten. He emphasizes that one of the main reasons for considering the subject at all is that any position which 'tends to promote the intensest possible orgasm in both partners simultaneously, or almost simultaneously, increases the probability of conception'.

Van de Velde divides his top ten into six Converse (face to face) positions and four Averse, which, poetically for him, he describes as the 'position of flight and pursuit'. Twenty-one pages of text are followed by four pages of tabular analysis, broken down into 'Type of Stimulation Afforded – To Woman; To Man': Indications: Contra-indications: For Conception. Here, very much truncated, is the gist:

CONVERSE POSITIONS

I. HABITUAL OR MEDIAL ATTITUDE

A.k.a. the Missionary. 'On the whole this attitude is both physiologically and psychologically appropriate. Psychologically, because it expresses the man's intense unconscious urge to *feel that he both protects and possesses* his partner, and equally, the *corresponding psychic needs* of the woman.' Not recommended for obese men. A 'medium degree' of stimulation – 'sufficient to bring about complete detumescence and relaxation of tension in both partners'. 'Apt' for conception.

2. ATTITUDES OF EXTENSION (Variation [a])

Ditto, except with woman's thighs closed. Good for 'phallic insufficiency'. Try it with a pillow under the woman. 'Less apt' for conception.

Suspensory (Variation [b])

Popular in Near East. Woman on edge of bed, feet on floor. Man standing diagonally. Good for stimulation, but 'arduous . . . inconvenient . . . exhausting'. Less apt for conception.

3. ATTITUDES OF FLEXION

Popular with Chinese. Woman on back; legs on man's shoulders. 'Suitable as a variation . . . but . . . has difficulties. Not every couple is capable of its gymnastic efforts.' Apt.

4. ATTITUDE OF EQUITATION (Astride)

'This is the method of coitus which the Roman poet Martial considered so normal and obvious that he could not conceive of that paragon of married couples, Hector and Andromache, in any other attitude.' Man on back, legs slightly bent. Woman astride and facing. 'Keenest possible excitement and gratification', though many women 'unable to learn or practise' position. But it means that man is completely passive – something 'directly contrary to the natural relationship of the sexes' which therefore 'must bring unfavourable consequences if it becomes habitual . . . Therefore, on these (profoundly psychological) grounds alone we cannot recommend the choice of this attitude in connection.' But good if man is tired. Not apt for conception.

5. SEDENTARY ATTITUDE (Vis-à-vis)

Man seated; woman suspended across his thighs. Both partners can move. Slight penetration, thus good during pregnancy. Less apt, on the whole.

6. ANTERIOR–LATERAL ATTITUDE (Sideways)

'Ovid describes the lateral attitude in the face to face position with these simple but adequate words: "Of love's thousand ways, a simple way and with least labour, this is: to lie on the right side, and half supine withal." ' Left side also possible. Convenient, and no pressure on woman, except leg. Good during convalescence. Man partialy immobilized. Apt.

AVERSE POSITIONS

7. PRONE OR VENTRAL ATTITUDE
Woman on front, man on top behind. 'Ventral attitude only possible for slim, lean people. Big buttocks ('ample adipose development of the female nates') or fatties ('appreciable abdominal corpulence in the man') an obstacle. Less apt, and therefore 'utilized by couples who would shrink from more active interference with natural processes'.

8. POSTERIOR–LATERAL ATTITUDE
The same, except with both partners on side. 'The least exhausting of any.' Most suitable for weak or ill partners or during pregnancy. Apt.

9. ATTITUDE OF FLEXION
Woman kneels, supported on hands and arms (see nymph in bronze group, 'Faun and Nymph', in the Museo Nazionale at Naples) or on a couch or chair (see 'wonderfully tender and absolutely decent drawing' by Gustav Klimt. Man kneels or stands. May cause 'unpleasantly suggestive and quite audible whistling sounds'. The process may be 'only too audible and extraordinarily repulsive in its effect'. Otherwise a popular variation, but preferred 'only because people "want something different", but have not clearly thought out *what* they want. So they simply choose the method which they observe to be usual in subhuman nature.' Rather apt.

10. POSTERIOR–SEDENTARY ATTITUDE
Man seated. Wife on top, with back turned. Can produce acute stimulation, but otherwise flawed. Not especially apt.

And that, I'm afraid, is more or less that. Subsequent writers come up with less starchy names – 'the spoons' . . . the 'Adam and Eve' position – though others match van de Velde for terminology, with Hutton talking of 'the habitual posture' and Parkinson-Smith referring to 'coitus a tergo'. Rear-entry to you. Alex Comfort adopts some French phraseology – 'croupade . . . cuissade . . . flanquette . . . negresse'. *More Joy of Sex* also contains one of the most enjoyable picture captions in all the available literature: 'Rear entry is a whole scene'. Wright claims the Missionary position for Europe, while Gochros and Fisher appropriate it as being 'as American as apple pie'. Marie Stopes chides men who refuse to allow anything but the Missionary approach, even though they can nearly suffocate their wives thereby.

But few improve significantly on the basic van de Velde categorizations and where they do it is more often than not a case of – in the words of the *Sun*'s guide – 'all that is different may be that an elbow is one foot lower'. This seems to be the case with *The Complete Book of Love and Sex*, which, like van de Velde, uses tabular form to illustrate no fewer than twenty-six positions – most of them variations on the Big Ten. The consumer is assisted in his or her choice by a handy Key to Symbols in the table: F – Couple can kiss; J – Needs little undressing; M – Stimulates G-Spot; O – Good for learning sex with new partner; R – Tiring. All that is missing are the Best Buy or Worth Thinking About categories.

Similarly, Jerome and Julia Rainer speak of there being hundreds of positions – 'one reliable figure is 206' – while at the same time conceding that 'many are, of course, near duplicates [and] some require the agility of trapeze artists to accomplish'. The Rainers devote two chapters to such variants, fetchingly entitled 'Antidotes to Monotony (1)' and 'Antidotes to Monotony (2)'. Together, say the Rainers, they amount to a 'kinesthesia of erotic pleasure' and 'something that lovers are not likely to come upon without instruction'.

The Rainers manage two or three dozen in all: it is difficult to be precise since so many are minor variants of others. The authors are particularly thoughtful in tailoring postures for husbands and wives who may be unorthodox in respective sizes. Thus such and such a posture serves admirably 'a corpulent wife and a lean husband' while 'an obese husband with protuberant stomach' might find such a one appropriate if wedded to a slender wife. 'When both spouses are corpulent, the most satisfactory are the posterior postures . . . a muscular husband and a petite wife may enjoy . . .' There are further combinations suitable for the bath, for the mechanically adjustable bed, for a chaise longue, for the husband who 'may sometimes choose to approach his drowsing wife', for couples possessing a high antique bed or sturdy chair without arms and, most spectacularly, couples with a swing. But, in cataloguing a standing position – the so-called 'clinging vine' – they do notch up a significant advance on the horizontally-minded van de Velde.

Tim and Beverly La Haye search, as ever, for Biblical authority, quoting from the *Song of Solomon*: 'Let his left hand be under my head and his right hand embrace me.' But they are broad-minded enough to consider three variants, while placing special emphasis on the importance of the bedboard: 'It is important to the husband to have his feet firmly against the foot of the bed or some solid object to aid him . . . In case of a bed that has no foot-board, the couple may reverse their position, placing his feet against the headboard.' Helen Gurley Brown is reserved about the need for lavish experimentation. 'If the missionary position is the one you truly enjoy, no need to keep working your way back and forth through the *Kama Sutra*.' Though she adds: 'Perhaps you had better work your way through it *once*, just to make sure you aren't missing anything.'

If that sounds a little lacking in spontaneity, console yourself with *The Joy of Sex*. Dr Comfort is in favour of planning sequences of postures, making as few extreme shifts as possible. He assures readers that, with practice, as many as twenty different postures a session will become automatic.

But even this sounds impulsive set alongside the sort of other recommendations for injecting variety into the act. Consider the intuitive artlessness of Marabel Morgan's five-part 'assignment' to keeping your husband guessing:

1. Be an atmosphere adjuster in the morning. Set the tone for love. Be pleasant to look at, be with, and talk to. Walk your husband to the car each morning and wave until he's out of sight.
2. Once this week call him at work an hour before quitting time to say: 'I wanted you to know that I just crave your body.' Then take your bubble bath shortly before he comes home.
3. Thrill him at the front door in your costume. A frilly new

nightie and heels will probably do the trick as a starter. Variety is the spice of sex.

4. Be prepared mentally and physically for intercourse every night this week. Be sure your attitude matches your costume. Be the seducer rather than the seducee.

5. If you feel your situation involves a deeper problem, either psychological or physiological, seek professional help.

Or try the Gochros/Fisher School of sexual ad-libbing: 'Ask your partner what items of clothing – bras, jockey shorts, gauze pants, garter belts, jock straps – really turn him or her on . . . if you have the time, resources and motivation, you can even get into costumes that fit your erotic fantasies – Western gear, Roman togas (converted bed sheets will do) or what have you.'

Alex Comfort is engagingly frank. Much of it really does come down to preparation with him. 'Nobody wants a seven-course meal every day,' he tells readers. The culinary metaphor from *Joy* is extended even further in *More Joy*: 'Think what meals would be like if neither of you had ever tasted anyone else's cooking.' 'Playtime' is one leavener in Dr Comfort's diet: 'Don't be scared of psycho-drama,' he advises. 'It works far better in bed than in an encounter group – Be the Sultan and his favourite concubine, the burglar and the maiden, even a dog and a currant bun.' At which point we start straying into the altogether more specialized area of fantasy. Woof, woof.

8

Friction and Fantasy

Fantasy has only recently been added to the curriculum of sexual studies. For a long time it was hardly mentioned at all save as something potentially destructive. You have only to look at how the anti-masturbators warned of the damaging, even perverted, consequences of over-straining the imagination. If discussed at all, fantasy was associated with a sub-culture of mandrake, yohimbine, opium, morphine, cocaine, hashish and hypnotism.

And then came some acknowledgement that erotic fantasy was not simply a by-product of alchemy, but something that could consciously be indulged in. This wasn't to be allowed. Sadler is sternly housemasterish in 1952 in decrying fantasies during intercourse: 'Marriage has become real now, and it is not necessary to employ a fantasy lover to secure sex satisfaction.' Nine years later Gilbert Oakley attacks as 'acts of impurity' and 'inverted and lustful' the reading of pornographic literature. Amongst the questions in his readers' questionnaire is one asking: 'Do you imagine yourself with another female when having intercourse with your wife?' You do? Then, says Dr Oakley, you have a 'promiscuous nature'. It shows 'that sex to you is not so much a matter of married happiness as an excuse to have intercourse'.

Since when most writers have come round to a view of sex as being, in Helen Singer Kaplan's phrase, 'composed of friction and fantasies'. But it was probably the appearance of Nancy Friday's collection of female fantasies, *My Secret Garden*, in 1973 that encouraged authors of sex manuals positively to embark on programmes of instruction in the technique of fantasy. Ms Friday herself had earlier met with strong resistance when she tried including women's fantasies in novel form, only to have it rejected by her (male) editor. 'When Henry Miller, D. H. Lawrence and Norman Mailer – to say nothing of Genet – put their fantasies on paper, they are recognized for what they can be: art,' she complains in *My Secret Garden*. 'The sexual fantasies of men like these are called novels. Why then, I could have asked my editor, can't the sexual fantasies of women be called the same? But I said nothing.' Jill Tweedie's foreword to the British edition two years later remarks: 'When I began to read the book I reacted much like many of the women who told Nancy Friday of their fantasies – hey, hey, fancy that. I have one like that too. So *that*'s a sexual fantasy.'

But in California the first video-aided course in fantasy was already out, with Nancy Friday duly featuring in its bibliography. Week One of the *Sexual Attitude Restructuring Guide* is accompanied by four videos – *Margo* ('Look for the orgasmic ripples after the first sharp spasm . . . the film of sweat over entire body'); *Shirley*; *Feeling Good*; and lastly *Unfolding*,` the scenario for which runs: '*Unfolding* explores the world of fantasy and the multiple images there. It is a search for fantasy fulfillment through memory reorganization and image transformation. Look for fantasy archetypes – images and patterns common to most people's fantasy and mythic worlds throughout history. Ask yourself, How many different kinds of sexual behaviour are there?' The next step – exercise in the book's fantasy programme – is to go out and buy two items of 'pornographic' material. Write about your reactions to it – is it 'an aphrodisiac, a moodshifter, a fantasy-starter'? Or neutrality, disgust, curiosity? On to exercise 8. Make up a fantasy. Time guide: ten minutes.

By the time you have reached Exercise 31 – Enrichment Through Fantasy – you are on the penultimate exercise of the whole book and should be well and truly unfolded. There are no fewer than twenty suggestions. Play with those that appeal to you:

'1. Spend an hour allowing your favorite sex images to appear on the screen in your mind. 2. Develop one of these images in great detail, conjuring up the environment, colors, smells, tastes, touches, sounds and textures . . . 4. Tell your fantasy to at least one other person. 5. Agree to spend some specific period of time acting on a fantasy with a partner . . . 7. Be a different sexual character for 24 hours. 8. Express yourself as a person of the opposite gender for 24 hours. 9. Read at least one piece of erotica or pornography . . . 12. Buy an object to improve your sexual image. 13. Make one positive comment about your sexuality to three people. 14. Have a sexual experience before dinner. 15. Write an ad for a lover. 16. Interview a consenting partner for the job of your

lover, master, slave, wife, husband. 17. Wear a costume to bed . . .
19. Masturbate while talking over the telephone to a consenting
friend. 20. Develop a detailed fantasy that incorporates your
personal sexual needs and your sexual politics.'

Everything is there bar the dog and the currant bun. And then there
is the reading to get through. Heiman and Lopiccolo's *Sexual Growth
Program for Women* offers an extensive and eclectic bibliography which
they see as 'a useful way of aiding sexual arousal and helping you to
clarify for yourself what does and does not turn you on.'

As well as a variety of magazines, including *Oui*, *Penthouse*,
Forum, *Playboy*, *Playgirl* and *Viva*, the authors suggest the following
reading list to be getting on with:

William Goldman: *Boys and Girls Together*
Maxwell Kenton: *Candy*
Harold Robbins: *The Carpetbaggers*
John Updike: *Couples*
Anaïs Nin: *Diary*
Pasternak: *Dr Zhivago*
John Cleland: *Fanny Hill*
Baudelaire: *Flowers of Evil*
Nancy Friday: *Forbidden Flowers*, *My Secret Garden*
Ayne Rand: *The Fountainhead*
Doris Lessing: *The Four-gated City*
D. H. Lawrence: *The Fox*, *Lady Chatterley's Lover*, *Sons and Lovers*,
   The Virgin and the Gypsy, *Women in Love*
John Fowles: *The French Lieutenant's Woman*
Puzo: *The Godfather*
Mary McCarthy: *The Group*
Xaviera Hollander: *The Happy Hooker*
Alex Comfort: *The Joy of Sex*, *More Joy of Sex*
Vatsayan: *Kama Sutra*
Frank Harris: *My Life and Loves*
Gore Vidal: *Myra Breckinridge*
Anon: *The Pearl*
Anon: *The Perfumed Garden of the Sheikh Nefzaoui*
Grace Metalious: *Peyton Place*
Shakespeare: *Romeo and Juliet*
R. Chartman: *The Sensuous Couple*
'J': *The Sensuous Woman*

Pauline Reage: *Story of O*
Scott Fitzgerald: *Tender is the Night*
Henry Miller: *Tropic of Cancer*
Jacqueline Susann: *Valley of the Dolls*

If, after all this, your imagination still thirsts for more, the authors suggest you go in search of ' "X-rated" movie theatres or adult bookstores near you that (may) provide some additional fantasy material. You may be surprised to discover just how much is available if you start pursuing these different sources of new information.'

Reassurance is at hand for those who fear the subterranean shadows that may be lurking as they roll back the rocks of reserve. 'If your fantasies involve doing something sexual with another woman, this does not automatically mean that you secretly prefer women as sexual partners,' say Heiman and Lopiccolo by way of example. Or, as Jane Cousins puts it: 'There's no limit to what people can fantasize about and there's no need to be scared about even quite violent fantasies . . . As long as you don't think you have to act out your wilder sex thoughts, there's nothing to worry about.' And, as for those who would ban sexy books and films – 'perhaps deep down what they're really complaining about is that people enjoy getting sexual feelings. But it's possible to be turned on by listening to classical music or by riding on a bus. No one has yet suggested that Beethoven or public transport should be banned.' Though some have tried to prune and privatize the latter.

By 1980 Gochros and Fisher are proclaiming fantasy 'a right'. It is also, they say a 'skill we can work on and improve'. Chapter 13 teaches you how to reach what must be considered post-graduate levels. We have another, albeit shorter, reading list – Jong, Nin, Tom Robbins, Lawrence, Sidney Sheldon, Comfort and, yes, Nancy Friday. Exercise 1 – do it with your partner or separately – involves writing or tape-recording some of your favourite fantasies. Exercise 2 – 'Window-shopping for Fantasies' – lists items that might arouse you. Get your partner to do the same. What about *erotic ideas* – group sex, watching someone else, past memories, dominating partner? What about *erotic places* – a beach in Hawaii, a fancy French hotel, in an elevator? What about *erotic times* – early in the morning, just after a nice dinner, while you're both watching a football game? What about *erotic situations* – meeting someone at an airport, sex in the back of a gas station with an attendant, under the table of a deserted restaurant with your waitress, hiding on a spaceship and having sex with an astronaut?

The final exercise involves stringing all these diverse elements into your own photofit fantasy. The sample multi-sensory experience conjured up by Gochros and Fisher gives an idea of the sort of thing to aim at – an amalgam of the best of Lawrence, Cartland and the correspondence columns of *Knave*: 'I'm walking through the forest preserve with my wife. We sit down on a bed of pine needles in the middle of a small grove of trees. We begin to make love. I feel her stroking my thighs, with her finger tips brushing over my penis. I feel a warm breeze over my chest – I am shirtless. When she kisses me I taste her lips . . . There's the unexpected element of making it in the woods high above the ocean in the distance. I imagine hearing her moan with pleasure as I enter her. We still have some of our clothes on . . . Being partly dressed, being outdoors, and doing it in broad daylight all really turn me on.' The location doubtless owes something to the authors' own situation as Professors at the University of Hawaii School of Social Work, but the highly trained imagination will have little difficulty in adapting the fundamental idea behind it.

Not that the traffic is all one-way. There is a plucky rearguard action against this New Cockaigne by Tim and Beverly La Haye in 1976 – one of the happy instances where Tim and Beverly are able to adduce a Biblical text, Matthew 5:28. ' "Fantasizing" about a woman other than your wife is a fancy title for old-fashioned "lust" which Jesus Christ equated with adultery,' they state unequivocally. More pragmatically, fantasizing 'tends to overstimulate, producing a premature ejaculation, and it creates unreal expectations. Just because something is exciting doesn't make it right.' A woman reader writes: 'Is it sinful to fantasize some illicit relations with another man during sex relations with my husband?' Tim and Beverly: 'You have developed a very bad mental habit. Transfer your thoughts to your husband . . . make love in a softly lighted room, keep your eyes open, and concentrate on what you are doing.'

Tim and Beverly offer six other steps for those who, light or no light, are still troubled:

1. Confess all evil thinking as sin – 1 John 1:9.
2. Walk in the spirit – Gal. 5:16–25.

3. Ask God for victory over the habit – 1 John 5:14,15.
4. Whenever possible, avoid all suggestive material – i.e., most movies, questionable TV programs, and pornography.
5. If you are married, think only of your wife or husband; if single, force your mind to think pure thoughts about all other people – Phil. 4:8.
6. Repeat the above steps when your mind digs up old lustful thought patterns.

The Tim and Beverly way is, it should be said, rather more time-consuming than the alternative – it takes 'from thirty to sixty days to create new thought patterns, so don't expect success overnight'.

And, finally, there are those who, while acknowledging the potency and value of fantasy, are nevertheless less sanguine about its nature and more reserved about some of the suggested aids. Sheila Kitzinger, in particular, thinks women should be aware of the implications of women's fantasies about being subjected to violence: 'Our fantasies are not isolated occurrences, detached from the rest of existence . . . Women seem to have fantasies about being dominated and brutalized, for example, far more than men do, and this mirrors something about the relations between men and women in our society.'

Nor is she very keen on the sort of soft pornography recommended by her colleagues in the field. Pornography, she says, not only causes violence, it *is* violence: 'The fantasy material on sale for men in newsagents typically depicts them overpowering women who are either virgins ('nymphets', schoolgirls and nuns) or whores (prostitutes and 'nymphomaniacs') and magazines like *Playboy* talk about sex using military metaphors – surrender, dominance and mastery . . . Because we live in a violent world in which women really are raped and battered by men, it is understandable that many of us feel bad about our masochistic fantasies.'

In *The Complete Book of Love and Sex* there is a further word of caution to those tempted to share their fantasies with their partners. 'If you do declare your fantasy it puts a tremendous pressure on your partner to accept it, because what you are really saying is, "This is the way I am, and you have to accept it all and not get angry or stop loving me." . . . Often the knowledge that one's partner really wants something one can't or won't supply can niggle away in the back of one's mind and work adversely in the relationship . . . To a woman the idea that her love should be judged by her willingness to dress up as a schoolgirl to have intercourse, for example, is outrageous. Few women want to hear about their men's fantasies for the girl next door because it arouses fears that fact and fiction might just become the same, given half a chance.'

Which, in reverse, is just what Nancy Friday herself found. She kicks off *My Secret Garden* by relating how, mid-intercourse with a lover, she shared with him the fantasy rushing through her mind at that moment – being rogered by an anonymous football supporter as they both stood in a cheering crowd watching George Best shoot at goal. The lover duly showed his appreciation by getting up and walking out.

'Where are you now, old lover of mine?' Ms Friday inquires poignantly. 'If you were put off by my fantasy of "the other man" what would you have thought of the one about my Great Uncle Henry's Dalmatian dog?' Nothing, one imagines, so innocent as currant buns.

9

Comings and Goings

The Orgasm was marketed and campaigned for so successfully in the 1960s and 1970s that it is perceived now as having been one of the primary innovations of that Periclean Age. *Cosmopolitan*'s monthly motif became the crusade for a woman's right to come. Pitiable were those condemned to have lived before this dawn! So panoramic was the general sense of enlightenment that even Tim and Beverly LaHaye were swept along by it. 'For centuries', they empathise in 1976, 'most married women did not experience orgasms frequently, and many never knew what orgasms felt like.' Not even Christians.

But disentangle from the hype of the Big O era and it becomes plain that the fashion in advice dolled out in sex manuals actually flows in just the opposite direction. Writers in the 1920s and 1930s are often startlingly fierce in their advocacy of the right – and, indeed, the need – of women to have orgasms at all costs whereas by the late 1970s and 1980s the whole subject is being treated with a weary nonchalance. 'Orgasms', sigh Gochros and Fisher in 1980, 'are not the be-all and end-all of sex.' And by 1980 one has to define what one means by sex.

All of which is not to deny the widespread ignorance that did exist – does still – so far as women's enjoyment of sex was and is concerned. Marie Stopes despairs, in *Married Love*, of her belief that 'from their published statements and their admissions to me it appears that many practising doctors are either almost unaware of the very existence of orgasm in women, or look upon it as a superfluous and accidental phenomenon.'

But while there may have been ignorance even amongst medical practitioners, there was no illusion amongst those considering themselves specialists as to the importance of the orgasm to women. 'To have had a moderate number of orgasms at some time at least,' writes Marie Stopes, 'is a necessity for the full development of a woman's health and all her powers.' She notes, for example, the prevalence of sleeplessness amongst women who have never had sex and deplores *coitus interruptus*, which left women in 'mid-air' and had 'a very bad effect on her nerves and general health'.

But this is pale stuff when set beside the thunderings of van de Velde eight years later. The lack of orgasm in women, he writes, causes 'ungratified jarring, nervous anger, fatigue, malaise and pain'. Once in a while it might do no permanent harm. 'But it is very different if and when the same disappointment is incessantly repeated. The congestion of the genitalia becomes chronic; frequently morbid discharges are set up; the functions of ovulation and menstruation become irregular, profusely painful or suppressed.' It was all a terrible waste of the services of gynaecologists and doctors.

Faced with any such situation, van de Velde's instinct is always to subject it to close analysis. He comes to the conclusion in *Ideal Marriage* that there are three predisposing causes for such an unhappy state of affairs – mechanical contraceptive barriers; the practices of *coitus reservatus* (where the man holds back from his orgasm) and *coitus interruptus*; and inadequate technique on the part of the male.

Van de Velde's objections to rubber barriers, whether sheaths or caps, and withdrawal methods stems from his belief that the vaginal (as opposed to clitoral) orgasm was at least partly triggered by male ejaculation. Orgasm *could* occur without it in the more excitable sort of woman but, he argues, 'it is equally certain that the man's ejaculation gives the signal for the woman's orgasm as well as his own.' This happened in two ways – either through 'realization of the muscular contractions of the man's orgasm; or from the impact of the vital fluid. In any case, the significance of the second is great: and the greater the more tender and fervent the woman's love.'

Van de Velde himself constructs what he believes to be the orgasmic experience of the majority of women. If they could be articulate on the subject, he thinks, they would say something along the following lines:

'After the accumulated tension of the preceding contacts and stimuli has brought me to a state of intense anticipation and excitement, I feel the onset of the orgasm at the precise instant that I perceive the first convulsive contractions of the phallos in the vulva and vagina, and simultaneously the orgastic spasms of my husband's whole body. The ecstasy of this supreme moment is such that its increase by further stimuli would be impossible and beyond my power to endure. Then – I feel the liquid torrent of the ejaculate – which gives a perfectly distinct sensation – as *gloriously soothing* and refreshing at the same time. It enables me to receive unimpaired delight and benefit from the concluding rhythmic ejaculatory movements, without over-strain. These stimuli, afforded by the masculine spasms, and the soothing libations of the seminal liquid are so complete and harmonious that my enjoyment remains at its summit, until my husband's orgasm ceases, when mine also very gradually and slowly subsides.'

So gloriously soothing does van de Velde consider seminal fluid that he warns that, should it be denied a woman, it 'may lead to excessive local irritation and congestion . . . One method of obviating this bad result is by psychic effort on the part of the woman, as by conscious contemplation of some other object. But if she neither can nor will do this she runs some risk in the long run, and in frequent intercourse, of local congestion and unrelieved tension which is far from negligible, whether physically or psychically, especially if there is an individual tendency to neuroses.'

Cases of inadequate technique were bad enough, as were the 'stupid and cruel selfishness' of men which led to them disregarding their wives' needs. But van de Velde reserves his special fury for *coitus interruptus*, or 'conjugal fraud', since it afforded the man some relief while leaving his wife unsatisfied. 'For the woman the effects of this practice are infinitely serious unless, indeed, she is without any sexual sensibility and remains "cold" and passive throughout the performance – which in such circumstances can only be considered fortunate.' He seeks to warn against it 'with all the emphasis at my command'. It could only be practised by men who cared nothing for their wives as individuals or mates. The cornerstones of such marriages would crumble, if they were not already in ruins. 'For sexually adequate, sensitive and vitally vigorous people, systematic *coitus interruptus* means not only a degradation but also an extermination of the marital relationship: a danger to the husband's health and a crime against the wife.'

So convinced is van de Velde of the physical necessity for women to have orgasms that he considers whether wives married to men who are unable to produce orgasms in them by genital friction should be allowed subsequently to use 'autotherapeutic measures'. Van de Velde is not the first to debate this matter. He notes that 'the older school of Catholic theologians' also discussed the inherent moral conflicts posed by it. The Vicar-General, D. Craisson, gave judgment in '*On Sexual Matters for the Guidance of Father Confessors*' (Paris, 1870), reporting that a greater number of moral theologians were in favour of frustrated wives behaving thus. Encouraged by this, van de Velde launches yet another passioned appeal to all husbands: 'So, above all I would impress on all married men; every considerable erotic stimulation of their wives that does not terminate in orgasm on the woman's part represents an injury, and repeated injuries of this kind lead to permanent – or very obstinate – damage to both body and soul.'

It is unlikely that such passionate pleadings ever found their way into *Cosmopolitan*, albeit that van de Velde's biology is more than a little eccentric, not to mention homocentric. Few subsequent writers place quite such emphasis on the role of male ejaculation in activating the female orgasms, though the distinction between vaginal and clitoral orgasms famously held sway for decades thereafter.

Van de Velde should not, of course, be held responsible for first drawing this distinction, though he advances it with some confidence. 'We must clearly understand that the sensations caused by the stimulation of the vagina are quite distinctive and dissimilar from those due to stimulation of the clitoris. In both cases there is pleasure, and characteristically sexual pleasure, or *voluptas*. But the sensations differ as much between themselves as the flavour and aroma of two fine kinds of wine.' He thinks the orgasms induced by clitoridal and vaginal stimulation 'curiously, though not widely, *different*', adding: 'Perfect and *natural* coitus should involve both types of stimulation.'

Under the van de Velde system of biology simultaneous orgasm is not only perfect and natural, but also commonplace since, as he is careful to explain, 'the time it takes for the sensation received by the woman to reach her central nervous system and translate itself into supreme delight *is less than a second*.' Later writers do not dwell on the biotechnology, but concur on the substantive question of the need for orgasms to coincide. Weatherhead, once more quoting his friend Dr Marion Greaves, says that 'in the perfect act these climaxes or orgasms should be simultaneous . . . a condition which is essential to a perfect experience.' No husband, in any event, should withdraw before his wife had a climax since this was 'exceedingly bad' for her nerves. Withdrawal before his own climax was simply pernicious. Havil goes still further: 'It is a nervous catastrophe of the first order for a woman to be left unsatisfied.' He thinks the ideal is 'that a man should ejaculate just when the woman has her orgasm . . . to this end, somewhat skilful cooperation is required.'

The emphasis on the simultaneous orgasm continues to be thundered home by writer after writer, though some take a realistic view of the likelihood of its happening every time. Parkinson-Smith advises synchroneity, but concedes that 'in actual fact the husband's often occurs before the wife's. But in no circumstances should he withdraw until he is sure that his wife's climax has been reached.' Hutton advises that 'the best results are obtained' from intercourse resulting in simultaneity. But 'if absolute synchroniza-tion cannot be arrived at, then the woman should at least have her orgasm before the man has his . . . if the woman does not arrive at orgasm then her sexual organs are left in a state of congestion which may take many hours to pass off. This may result in a more or less chronic state of congestion of the organs with harmful side effects.' Hutton is, however, against too frequent manual stimula-tion where more natural means have failed – 'it is a rudimentary act resembling self-stimulation and is far removed from the mutual synchronized adult vaginal form of sexual intercourse.'

But set against this consistent strand there are already voices of pragmatism and dissent. Exner's aspirations on behalf of woman-kind are considerably more modest than some of his colleagues', arguing that no serious effects would be sustained in women who had orgasms in a minimum of 20 per cent of 'couplings'. MacAndrew offers similarly calm counsel: 'Women who do not obtain orgasm should not feel themselves outcasts or abnormal. Many successful wives have never had a single orgasm, but have cooperated and experienced pleasure in intercourse.'

But Eustace Chesser is much more radical still in 1941, disagreeing that orgasm, still less simultaneous orgasm, is an essential component of love-making. ' "Why do I never experience orgasm?" an anxious wife asked after two years of marriage,' he begins his chapter, 'The Meaning of Orgasm', in *Woman and Love* (1962). 'That same question has been asked a hundred times over.

Before attempting a reply another question should be put: "Do you enjoy intercourse?" If the answer is "Yes" there is little need to pursue the matter further. To worry about orgasm is quite unnecessary. A technical term has somehow gained currency and many of those who use it do not know what it means.'

Rather than speak of 'orgasm', urges Chesser, 'it would be wiser to speak of sexual satisfaction. We know that pleasure can vary in intensity. Some people go into transports of ecstasy over simple experiences that produce only mild enjoyment in others . . . It is not a question of doing some mechanical work the right or wrong way.'

This was no more than a continuation of the line Chesser had taken more than twenty years earlier in *Love Without Fear*: 'As we know, many women never experience orgasm, but nonetheless derive the greatest pleasure from love play and intercourse . . . Many a woman is unable to tell you whether or not she has ever experienced orgasm, for the simple reason that its intensity seems to vary considerably.'

Future writers generally take their tone from Chesser. The emphasis on simultaneous orgasm is 'ridiculous nonsense', says 'J'. Brown and Faulder agree: 'Sometimes it does happen, and when it does it can be an exceptionally moving experience, but more often it does not and it really is not important, provided that both partners are satisfied by their love-making and are orgasmic at the moment when they are ready for it.'

Jane Cousins is one of many to dispose of the vaginal/clitoral distinction. She does so *en route* to attacking the apostles of the simultaneous orgasm – something that 'rarely happens, and if it does it isn't necessarily the great thing some people make it out to be. It's fine if you like it. But if you're so involved in your own orgasm, you might not get the rather special pleasure of seeing your partner come.' Gone are the fearsome medical consequences of not coming that van de Velde's women readers learned to anticipate: 'It's important to realize that not everyone has an orgasm every time they have sex. This is perfectly normal and there's no reason why it should be seen as a failure. It can sometimes be very frustrating not to come, but sex isn't just about scoring "comes".'

The new consensus is well-established by the 1980s. To Heiman and Lopiccolo simultaneity can be positively detrimental by putting too much pressure on the aspiring participants. Ditto *The Complete Book of Love and Sex*: 'The intense psychological, physical and emotional effort needed to have simultaneous orgasms is so great for most couples that it actually detracts from their enjoyment of intercourse . . . it is not worth striving for it as an end-point.' Nowinski blames D. H. Lawrence: 'A romantic notion of the 20th century is that when two people are truly in love with each other they will reach orgasm at the same time. . . . The ability to have simultaneous orgasms becomes a test of a relationship. This ideal is clearly expressed in *Lady Chatterley's Lover*.'

Gochros and Fisher think orgasms 'great . . . but not essential . . . A great deal of pleasure and fulfillment can be obtained sexually without the need for orgasms.' Nor is one 'type' of orgasm more or less mature than another. Got that, Sigmund? Alex Comfort says it's so much hogwash, too. And, as for him, coming together's fine but he considers it a modern sexual hangup to expect it every time or even often. Or, as Helen Gurley Brown has it, 'There is so much else to do in bed than peak.'

All this reassurance is most comforting, but nonetheless confusing when set alongside the acres of advice on achieving the potential of orgasm offered – forgive me – simultaneously. In some part this must be a reaction against the boastfulness of the earlier sex manuals in appropriating for men the sole credit and responsibility for orgasm in women. Who needs men? Who needs intercourse? The new biological truth dawned that conventional coupling was actually a moderately inefficient way of producing orgasms, if that *was* what women were supposed to want and need so badly. 'This', explains Sheila Kitzinger in 1983, 'is why many women have better orgasms while masturbating, for example, than with intercourse . . . Women making love to each other sometimes discover that each of them has more orgasms than in lovemaking with men.' Equally threateningly for men, she advises women who are not gaining the sort of satisfaction they are seeking to try changing tempo or position – or, failing that, 'it may mean changing the partner.'

'Orgasm has been set up by our culture as something women should strive for, as a gift men must offer women and the proof of sexual success for both partners. For most women, orgasm does not have this central role in life. And if it does, it tends to be for a small part of their lives . . . When a woman is persuaded that she ought to want orgasms or that she could have better orgasms, or more of them, the pressure to perform sexually, to achieve, to excel, is often just one more stress in a life already burdened with difficulties in sorting out relationships, serving others and finding space to be herself. For some women lovemaking without orgasm is unsatisfying and they feel they have missed out on something precious. For others the journey holds more richness and delight than the getting there. For others again, the love they feel for another human being contains a deeper satisfaction even than orgasm.'

Sexual Myth Number One out of a dozen compiled by Gochros and Fisher reads: 'Sex is essentially intercourse.' 'Remember,' they add, 'there is no reason why each sexual activity has to climax with a penis in your vagina – unless your goal is to get pregnant.' Chapter 10 in Heiman and Lopiccolo's book, *Becoming Orgasmic*, is headed 'Intercourse – Another Form of Mutual Pleasure'. Almost an afterthought to earlier chapters on getting to know yourself, exploration by touch, touching for pleasure (parts one and two), using a vibrator ('A little help from a friend') sharing self-discovery with a partner and pleasuring each other.

Heiman and Lopiccolo want to see you be more flexible. Re-evaluate your feelings about intercourse and orgasm during intercourse. Try a few sessions that exclude intercourse altogether. 'One advantage of the alternatives is that they reduce feelings of pressure to have orgasm during intercourse.' Chapter 11 proceeds to outline some of the non-intercourse, non-penetrative alternatives, which include prominently oral sex.

The apparent increase in the sum total of oral sex being indulged in the West is attributed by *The Complete Book of Love and Sex* to male confusion over his role in a world of declining intercourse. 'Maybe', the authors speculate, 'the male population collectively is losing its self-confidence with regard to penile performance and is increasingly depending on the more reliable tongue, which does not lose its erection or come too quickly.'

It must be said that the male orgasm doesn't get much of a look in amidst all this sisterly welter of clashing ideologies. But there is the odd sprinkling of counsel here and there for men still engaging in the more old-fashioned by-ways of sex – most of them to do with hanging on long enough. There is, as touched on already, the technique of self-distraction. 'Some have suggested that men during intercourse may profitably contemplate nonstimulating things,' as Tim and Beverly LaHaye put it – 'sport, business, or, as one husband said, "I think about paying the monthly bills."'

Well, OK, but just don't overdo it, say Tim and Beverly. Unlike van de Velde, who is rather against the notion, thinking it an abuse when a husband 'has recourse to artificial means of distracting his attention, such as eating, drinking, smoking, etc., as well, of course, as consciously directing his thoughts away from his sensations.'

A doctor, happily named Semans, is credited with the development of the 'squeeze' technique for delaying orgasm in males in 1959, later modified by Masters and Johnson and widely recommended ever since. Then there is the art of Karezza, practised by the Oneida community (established in the NY State town of that name between 1851 and 1876) and explored at some length by Marie Stopes, amongst others. Some writers seem a little confused as to what it actually is, but, as defined by the American gynaecologist Dr Robert Latou Dickinson, it is 'Prolonged intercourse, accompanied by maximum and varied excitement, with orgasm for the woman if desired; with no seminal emission – or rare external emission – but with the substitution of a gradual subsidence of feeling for the man.'

Dr Stopes is impressed by the spiritual aspects of the technique, though she thinks it unlikely that 'an average, strong and unimaginative Englishman' would be up to it. Chesser disagrees, and devotes eight pages to it in *Love Without Fear*. 'Experience has convinced me that prolonged coital play is by no means beyond the powers of the average married couple . . . Many have informed me that they have found this method ideally suited to their needs in middle years . . . The gentle prolonged intercourse of Karezza tends to appeal to woman's emotional attitude. The very fact that the husband is deliberately holding himself in check, and is finding his own happiness in seeking, above all else, to ensure hers, is a powerful factor in drawing forth a response from the wife's deepest nature.'

Van de Velde, on the other hand, thinks Karezza so much dangerous nonsense and feels he 'must utter an urgent warning' against it while at the same time ticking off Dr Stopes for apparently approving of it – she is 'an able – even an eminent person – [who has arrived] at absurd conclusions when venturing on territory in which she is not at home'. He goes so far as to deplore her use of the title 'Dr' (she was a D.Sc and D.Phil) on the grounds that the 'layman attributes undue weight to [her views] because of the supposed professional knowledge of the authoress.'

More recently, Karezza is one of a clutch of such techniques discussed in *Any Man Can* (1985) which offers to teach men to achieve the same capacity for multiple orgasm as is available to women. Yes, men have rights, too. The authors, Dr William Hartman and Marilyn Fithian, bemoan the deluge of literature on female sexuality – enough, they say, 'to make many normal men give up in despair . . . How much motivation can there be for a man to enter into sexual encounters that demand hours of work on his part – with only a few moments of pleasure as his reward?' The answer is obligingly supplied: 'Very little'.

Any Man Can sets out to correct a 'dismally unequal situation': 'We're talking about men sharing in the delights of having one orgasm after another.' The important thing is to begin by doing away with the fuddy duddy old belief that there should be an inextricable link between male orgasm and ejaculation. That there isn't was confirmed to Messrs Williams and Fithian's satisfaction by their laboratory experiments 'when 33 different men claimed that they were multi-orgasmic'.

Do not imagine we are talking about a piece of cake here, though. 'Don't assume that because others have multiple orgasms they can be achieved without effort,' warn the authors. 'Do you desire to learn this skill? Are you motivated to achieve your goal? Do you have the time to develop this skill?' Or, to put it another way, do you want to end up like Harry, a swinger on the US swinger circuit who was emphatically mono-orgasmic? In the memorable words of a fellow-swinger: 'As soon as Harry shoots his wad, he's finished.'

Poor old Harry. If only he had read up on some of the other assorted methods cited in *Any Man Can* – The Tao of Loving, the Tantra, Vajroli, Coitus Prolongatus, Vishrati, Coitus Obstructus, Imsak, Maithuna and so forth, many of them relying on the development of those old PC muscles. The authors are able to recommend two brands of 'masturbation machine' (made by Funways Inc.) to assist the handicapped or elderly in the learning process ('Don't set the machine at too high a speed') while Tim and Beverly LaHaye will be interested to learn that Hartman/ Fithian claim even to be able to produce evidence of Biblical masters of the multiple orgasm – in particular, King David, who was said to have had intercourse thirteen times in succession during the course of a single evening. Furthermore, Samson, a prolific shooter of his wad according to the authors, 'resembles one multi-orgasmic man we have observed in the laboratory'. Well, their research began in the sixties when long hair was the fashion. Latterday equivalents of Samson and David are authoratatively stated by the book to include Errol Flynn and Gary Cooper.

All that remains is to consider the difficult question, 'to fake or not to fake?' – a question hitherto only asked of women, though we may have to accustom ourselves to demanding it of contemporary Samsons and Davids. The balance is against faking, so we should perhaps look at the arguments in favour of it first.

These are most eloquently put by 'J', who tells her readers that 'every now and then the Sensuous Woman finds it necessary to pull out of her bag of pleasure one of her top skills – The Sarah Bernhardt. She Acts . . . If you do it well, he won't be able to tell. Surprising, I know, but true.' The three arguments for these thespian endeavours advanced by 'J' are as follows: '1. You make him happy; 2. A happy lover comes back again, and the next time you will probably be wild with passion and can hardly wait to make love; 3. Sometimes, if you are really a proficient actress, you fake yourself right into a *real* orgasm.'

This requires homework. 'To become a fabulous fake, study again every contortion, muscle spasm and body response that leads up to and makes up the orgasm and rehearse the process privately until you can duplicate it.' The only rule to observe is that 'you must *never*, *never* reveal to him that you have acted sometimes in bed. You will betray a trust shared by every other female in the world if you do.'

Chesser seems to have changed his mind on the subject in the twenty-one years that separate *Love Without Fear* and *Woman and Love*. In the former he considers that '*Simulation of orgasm* is within the power of any intelligent woman. Eve, who proves so adept in the practice of feminine arts which harmlessly deceive the male, can, once her eyes are opened to the need, simulate orgasm so well that it is almost impossible for the man to detect that genuine orgasm has not occurred.' Stand that on its head and you have Chesser Mark II: 'The wife who thinks she is flattering her husband by pretending to a satisfaction she does not feel will betray herself unless she realizes how she should react and look.

Only a very unsophisticated partner would be deceived by her feigned transports of delight.'

Geldenhuys is against it. Jane Cousins thinks 'there's absolutely no point. For a start it's nothing more than a lie and a dishonest trick. And if you go on faking you may never learn what it takes for you to have an orgasm.' The *SAR Guide* agrees: 'The energy expended and wasted in faking could be channeled into experiencing the moment-by-moment pleasure we are receiving.' Sheila Kitzinger is also against it, and thinks it nonsense to suggest that faking might eventually help a woman to have a real orgasm – 'These and similar theories about female sexuality derive from a male-dominated and directed therapy which perceives women's psycho-sexual experiences as basically stemming from, and a distortion of, a male model of sex.' Alexandra Penney has a more pragmatic objection: 'He'll never learn what really turns you on if you fake. "My husband thought he was a great lover," says one woman, "until he had an affair with a woman who let him know that he was not and taught him what he needed to know." '

The issue is altogether more complicated to Helen Gurley Brown's way of thinking: 'I think faking is like using drugs – Okay *sometimes*, but you don't want to depend on it/them. I can't imagine not faking *ever* . . . a woman can *pretend* the "display" then later, alone, really finish everything; nobody has to know at the time you didn't "make good" . . . At any rate, after someone has made love to you with skill and grace, an orgasm is a way of saying you enjoyed yourself, even as you compliment a host on a wonderful spinach quiche. A man is supposed to be able to *tell* when you are faking, but I don't think any man can *physically* tell. How could he? I have never been with a man who couldn't be "faked with".

'Listen, now that Shere Hite has corroborated that most of us have orgasms *not* by penetration, but by clitoral stimulation, and if enough men *know* that, or we *tell* them, we can now have more orgasms *during* lovemaking and faking won't be so necessary. Happy ending.'

And she, editor-in-chief of *Cosmopolitan* during the Big-O years, should presumably know.

10

Ripe Months, Autumn Years

A word for men: Having shot your wad do not then fall asleep. Remember your van de Velde. What stage follows the sexual union? The Afterglow. Precisely. It is, you will recall, 'an essential and most significant act in the love-drama'. And yet there are men – many men, according to *Ideal Marriage* – who skip it in favour of sleep. 'Yes, even men who *love* their wives do this sometimes, from ignorance or negligence.'

Listen to how van de Velde describes them: 'They turn round and presently lie torpid and snoring, while their wives feel the slow ebb of sexual longing, and thus they deprive themselves of the most exquisite psychic and emotional experiences, and they also destroy the illusions of the most loving wife, by showing that they have no idea of the woman's nature, of the aesthetic delicacy of her love, of the profound appreciation sexual pleasure arouses in her, of her need for caresses and sweet words, which lasts much longer than the orgasm. This is a closed book to them. In after-play the man proves whether he is (or is not) an *erotically civilized adult*.'

It is not a pretty picture, yet it is one that several writers feel it right to sketch, if not quite so graphically. Isabel Hutton numbers amongst her three cardinal rules for men: 'Don't roll over and start snoring immediately after a climax with your wife.' Marie Stopes stresses the *extreme* importance of 'close and prolonged contact after the culmination takes place . . . The benefit to both of the pair of remaining in the closest possible physical contact for as long a time as is possible after the crisis is almost incalculable.'

Eustace Chesser claims at least to understand the temptation to snooze: 'Let us be honest and admit that many men experience the desire to sleep as soon as orgasm has been attained. A woman rarely feels the same way and so she feels hurt when, culmination reached, she no longer matters.' It doesn't take much to prevent that wounded feeling setting in: 'A kiss, a tender embrace, loving words – all these will help a wife to feel that she is genuinely loved and not wanted for her body alone.' There are, of course, certain logistical problems encountered by couples with separate beds. Chesser is of some help here: 'When a couple have separate beds, it is far better for the man to remain with his wife for a while after congress . . . Of course, if lovers go to sleep in each other's arms, the fact that the man may fall asleep before his wife does not matter nearly so much, The maternal instinct, and all her loving affection, will go out to the man sleeping like a child on her breast.'

No guidance is, alas, offered as to the more complicated logistics involved in Emma Drake's advice in 1901 that married couples should inhabit, not simply separate beds, but separate rooms: 'The custom in many English homes of each having a room, which is peculiarly one's own, may seem to our freedom-loving natures a cold custom; but is not this better when a proper self-control seems difficult, than a freedom which degenerates into licence? True, the door between these two rooms should seldom be shut, but the fact that there are two rooms relieves of many temptations, and prevents the familiarity which even in married life, breeds contempt.'

What of sexual union during menstruation, something forbidden by Mosaic law but not, according to the more recent doctrinal advice offered by Tim and Beverly LaHaye, to be thought sinful today providing it is initiated only by the wife? Most writers seem to think it permissible, if slightly distasteful. Sheila Kitzinger states that there has never been any evidence to support the Jewish notion that menstruating women are unclean and points out that it may help to relieve menstrual tension, while Elizabeth Blackwell is one of the earliest to acknowledge what Alex Comfort so pithily expresses some ninety years later – that menstruation 'may be the girl's randiest time'.

But it would be a shame to have unanimous agreement on any such topic and so it is that we turn, for contrast, to Leslie Weatherhead's citation of 'leading authorities' – whether doctors or art historians he does not let on – who 'now agree that sexual intercourse, while harmless, should not, for aesthetic reasons, take place during menstruation'. Should you want medical grounds, though, Dr Gilbert Oakley is quite happy to supply them. Sex during menstruation is, he states confidently, 'Most *unsafe* for the husband, for he may well contract an unpleasant condition on his member through having contact with the menstrual flow which is, after all, poison leaving a woman's body. This is not hygienic practice, and appeals more to the baser instinct than to anything else.'

Dr Sperry displays a similar command of anatomical function in turning the question on its head: what happens to the menstrual cycles of women unfortunate enough to have been exposed to 'excessive use of the sexual organs?' The answer is that they frequently become abnormal. 'Sexual abuses and excesses undermine, debilitate, disease and kill thousands of our women annually,' he proclaims. 'Abnormally amorous, selfish and brutal husbands are prolific causes of sickly wives.'

But any dispute over sex during menstruation is but a timid paradox set beside the hand-to-hand fighting in the more serious war over sex during pregnancy, in which medicine is once more wrenched shamelessly to the aid of the respective combatants.

Harelip, cleft palate, mental deficiency, idiocy, mania or moral depravity – these are just some of the conditions Sperry thinks it 'reasonable to attribute' to 'lustful practices' during pregnancy. 'As soon as pregnancy is known to exist the couple should discontinue sexual indulgence and cease all lusting after carnal things. If possible a better domestic atmosphere than usual should pervade the house.'

But then Sperry is against many things during pregnancy – such as going to the circus. A mother-to-be, in his view, is, in effect, 'building a temple for an immortal soul' and should be nourishing that soul by visits to churches, libraries, art galleries, concerts, lectures 'and kindred edifying and purifying influences'.

Art galleries are especially important during the first two months of pregnancy, according to Emma Drake, who offers a month-by-month breakdown of the development of the foetus. The physical nature is formed during the first two months – so this is the time to 'study perfect pieces of statuary'. The evidence for this is to be found in Italy, where 'many of the native children bear a striking resemblance to the pictures of the child Jesus, from the adoration which the mothers give the Madonnas'. So probably best to steer clear of Dianne Arbus or Brueghel. The third and fourth months determine the 'vital instincts'; the perceptive powers are formed during the fifth and sixth months; from then on the humanitarian instincts take shape. Dr Drake's book, it should be noted, carries the endorsement of eight eminent Americans, including four clerics and a professor of gynaecology.

The foetus being impressionable in this way, Dr Drake thinks sex 'certainly can have no wholesome influence upon the unborn child, and assuredly not upon the love and respect which the wife feels for the husband . . . Study the question as I will, I can see no law or reason which justifies the husband in approaching the wife for the purpose of sexual gratification at any time during pregnancy.'

Dr Drake duly proceeds to an alarming illustration of the dangers of such gratification, culled from a book by a medical colleague entitled *Stirpiculture* – the breeding of pure races. It concerns a mother who gives birth to two children. During the first pregnancy her husband 'lovingly consented to let me live apart from him during the time I carried this little daughter under my heart . . . These were the happiest days of my life.' The resultant baby was 'like an exquisite rosebud – the flower of pure sanctified, happy love. She never cried at night, was never fretful or nervous, but was all smiles and winning baby ways, filling our hearts and home with perpetual gladness . . . I have never had the slightest difficulty in bringing her up. She has given me only comfort . . . the reason of all this is because my little girl had her birthright.'

The woman's second pregnancy is quite a different affair, since her husband 'had become contaminated with the popular idea that even more frequent relations were permissible during pregnancy. I was powerless against this wicked sophistry and was obliged to yield to his constant desires. But how I suffered and cried; how wretched I was.' The boy subsequently born 'after nine of the most unhappy, distressing months of my life' is a 'sickly, nervous fretting child – myself in miniature – and after five years of life that was predestined by all the circumstances to be just what it was, after giving us only anxiety and care, he died, leaving us sadder and wiser. I have demonstrated to my own abundant satisfaction that there is but one right, God-given way to beget and rear children, and I know that I am only one of many who can corroborate this testimony.'

Dr Drake concedes that there is the occasional wife who 'during pregnancy is troubled with a passion far beyond what she has ever experienced at any other time. This in every instance is due to some unnatural condition, and it should be considered a disease, and for it the physician should be consulted.' Any husband worthy of the title 'protector' had a role to play with a wife diseased in this way: 'Nowhere can he prove more loyally his love and respect for her, than in the tender appreciation which he shows her in the control of her own person. Nay, more than yielding simply to her wishes, he should be the leader in these things if necessary, and guide her into the stronger way.'

This is alarming stuff and would, one imagines, make a due impression on the newly married young wives it is aimed at. But the alarm could scarcely match the confusion of any young wives who read Dr Drake in conjunction with Marie Stopes's *Radiant Motherhood*, a book which takes Dr Drake's theories, stands them on their head and then proceeds to pull them inside out.

Marie Stopes's own ideas about sex and pregnancy developed from the letters she received in the wake of *Married Love* – a book which avoided a dogmatic statement of opinion on the subject. 'The women themselves were ashamed, almost humiliated, to confess that during the carrying of their child they most ardently desired unions.' Dr Stopes investigated the letter writers and was struck that they were 'almost without exception, the *best* type' – the sort that she would have supposed would have maintained a fierce chastity during the nine months on account of their purity, self-restraint and cultured natures.

Marie Stopes combines this data with other evidence concerning the properties of sperm. 'Now there is much evidence that in unmarried women, and in young wives who are debarred from sex union altogether, something approaching a subtle form of starvation occurs; conversely that women absorb from the seminal fluid of the man some substance, "hormone", "vitamine" or stimulant which affects their internal economy in such a way as to benefit and nourish their whole systems.

'If, therefore, the woman who is becoming a mother, and who is supporting a second life, feels the need of union with her husband it is, I maintain, an indication that her nature is calling out for something not only legitimate but positively beneficial and required, and it should be not only a man's privilege, but his delight, to unite with his wife at such a time and under such circumstances.

'The maintenance of the right balance of the internal secretion of the various glands which react on sex activity is important at all times, and particularly during the time when a woman is becoming a mother. One of the results of the growth of the child is the increased activity of the thyroid gland in the neck, which considerably increases in size.'

Dr Stopes considers that in the example of these fine women 'one has a guide for what is best for the race . . . an indication of the truest and highest standard of all.' It is furthermore during these 'brief sacred months' (the woman should require sex only infrequently, and not to orgasm) that the father, mother and baby are united in a 'profound mystical symbol'.

Dr Drake does not have the monopoly on alarm. Dr Stopes's work inclines her to the view that 'mothers whose natural desire for union has been denied, and mothers who are congenitally frigid rather tend to produce children with unbalanced sex-feeling liable to yield to self-abuse.' While, on the other hand, she quotes the example of a young man who makes love with his wife on the eve of her giving birth. The man tells Dr Stopes: 'Now our baby is one of the finest babies from all points of view.' And Dr Stopes, who has seen photographs of the child, 'can endorse the parent's opinion'.

One cannot, hand on heart, claim that Dr Stopes has a more fundamental grasp of anatomical workings than either Dr Sperry or Dr Drake. But it is nevertheless broadly Dr Stopes's view of the matter that prevails thereafter. Van de Velde confesses that, as a doctor, he has to advise against union during pregnancy, but that as someone with a little knowledge of life, he is all for it. 'For me there is no doubt at all. The reasons in *favour* of continued coitus during gestation are far more imperative and profound than those against it.' And one of the reasons is that he declares it 'nothing less than impossible for a man accustomed to active sexual life to stop complete functional satisfaction, more or less suddenly, for several months, and nevertheless to continue to play the wooer to his wife: to repeat the approaches of the prelude (which will mightily increase a sexual excitement that has become clamant through enforced abstinence), and then, again and again, to break off. No; and again no!'

The debate thereafter is solely in terms of the stage intercourse should cease – Weatherhead says eight months; MacAndrew, Hutton and Parkinson-Smith seven, with a variety of positions explored. The *Sun* Guide meanwhile seeks to reassure wives that hubby won't stop fancying them while they're in the club: 'He relishes that bump and, usually, the more sumptuous breasts that develop with it!' Well, she must know he doesn't read the *Sun* for its Law Reports.

So much for the pregnant months: what of what Tim and Beverly LaHaye refer to as the September Years? How long can one reasonably expect to – be expected to – keep going? We know already that there are those 'too old at forty' through their earlier excesses. 'A Physician' warns that woman's sexual life ends abruptly at the change of life – 'between the age of 45 and 50'.

Sperry advises easing up gradually during the years before the menopause 'During this transition period sexual intercourse should be carefully limited – or, perhaps, totally suspended.' Fear not, this will be no great imposition: 'Usually the desire for copulation gradually decreases and finally dies with the cessation of ovulation and menstruation; sometimes, however, desire for sexual excitement increases. This is abnormal, and should not be indulged.'

No such hard and fast rules apply with men. For one thing, the age of decline varies from land to land. 'In this country at the present time,' writes Sperry, an American, 'the age at which sexual desire and power are most likely to disappear is somewhere between the 40th and the 60th year. There are many who use up their sexual energies before passing the half century line. It is claimed that, on the average, the Englishman retains his virility ten years longer than the average native born American retains his.' Much depended on the sort of life one had led while younger: 'Vital capital that is squandered in early life cannot be recovered later for use in old age . . . Sexual abuse and excess, or sensuality in any form, lead to premature old age, to decay of body and mind, and to the abortion of that soul development.'

Rennie MacAndrew in 1928 provides a number of most thoughtful hints for those in the autumn years, by which time (over fifty-five) he thinks they might safely think of dabbling say once a fortnight or perhaps monthly. 'A woman with badly drooping breasts', for instance, 'might desire to wear her brassier. These may now be had in attractive flesh pink colour with an opening through which a small portion of breast can protrude. On the other hand, a good tip for the wife with fallen breasts is what might be called the Right Arm Trick. The arm is brought up under the bosom so as to raise it and make it firm. This makes the husband feel he is in the arms of a young girl with firm breasts, thus taking him back in memory to the happy early-married days.' The illusion is further helped by paying regard to another MacAndrew tip: 'If a man or woman shows any bodily defects, such as varicocele, or a drooping breast, no notice should be taken of it, for though its owner may not say so, there may be extreme sensitiveness about trifling malformations.'

If all this sounds a little grim, then so does the breezy here's-your-medicine-Mr-Smith tone adopted to cheer Autumn folk on their way. 'Rubbish,' Dr Chesser tells us he has exclaimed at a 44-year-old woman patient: 'Some of the best years of life lie ahead.' Tim and Beverly record a 76-year-old man boasting of his thrice-weekly exploits: 'Now that I'm retired we have more time for that sort of thing.' A Dutch survey quoted in *The Complete Book of Love and Sex* claims to show that 33 per cent of those over ninety still have an interest in sex, though only 3 per cent manage to translate this into practice involving a fellow senior citizen. A similar survey in America contradicts Sperry's claims: 'Those men who had been most sexually active in their early years remained the most active in their later years.'

'Be resourceful and imaginative in finding ways round problems as they arise, for example with arthritis,' chivvy the *Complete Book* authors: 'Ignore what people say about sex being only for the young.' Sex aids may help. The *Sun* Guide suggests trying its own section of sensate focus exercises titled How to Increase Your Sex Drive: 'after you have spent a week getting in touch daily with your own feelings then you can start doing the sensate focus exercises together . . . using a little cream or oil, massage and stroke one another all over.'

Alex Comfort advises his more mature readers of the importance of not dropping sex for any long period and to go it alone if temporarily without a partner. Those who get out of practice may have trouble re-starting, he warns. Sheila Kitzinger, by contrast, is rather severe on those who tell older women that they will atrophy if they don't have regular sex. *The Complete Book of Love and Sex*, pondering the same area, decides that, since men on the whole die rather earlier than women, bigamy might be a solution for people over a certain age. This would be unlikely to appeal to Tim and Beverly LaHaye, who turn their minds to just this question of what a widowed or divorced person can do 'to control his/her sex drive'. They offer six tips to a recently widowed woman who, until her husband died in a road crash, had been used to as many as ten orgasms a week. The woman, say Tim and Beverly, needed to know that:

1. God's grace is sufficient even for her need (2 Cor. 12:9);
2. Her stimulated desire would ease considerably in time with disuse;
3. She must guard her thought life carefully by Bible reading and prayer;
4. She must avoid all suggestive or compromising situations with the opposite sex;
5. She should become active in a local church and trust God to (a) supply another person with whom she can share her love need, or (b) give her the self-control to cope with her problem (1 Cor. 10:13); and
6. She could ask God to take away the craving (1 John 5:14, 15).

Tim and Beverly tell of another man, widowed after seventeen years of marriage, who 'confessed to a severe problem at first. He finally prayed earnestly that God would help him, and God removed that strong drive for six years. When he met another lady who finally became his wife, his normal appetite for lovemaking was quickly revived.'

Specialist books are a recent trend. *Enjoy Sex in the Middle Years* takes the riper reader through chapters on attitudes, family life, work, coping with sexual changes, difficulties, contraception and 'solo' ('nothing to be ashamed about'.) A section on positions explores the most suitable variants for those with back trouble/ rheumatism/weight problems/piles/arthritis or simply recovering from heart attacks. The line drawings are of suitably furrowed couples, supplemented, where appropriate, by photographs of distingué men flecked with grey apparently married to rather younger, jollyish women.

There is, inevitably, a video available for those who find such illustrations a trifle static. The *SAR Guide* film, 'A Ripple in Time', is devoted to a September couple who have evidently taken on board many of the sexual lessons of a more recent generation: 'The man is sixty-five; the woman fifty-two. They are taking their time. The woman pleasures herself during intercourse with a vibrator and with her hand.' The couple proceed through a variety of positions, with, to judge from the synopsis, a certain amount of encouragement needed, whether because of the man's advanced years or the inhibiting influence of the video camera it is not plain. But, hey presto!, viewers are eventually the privileged witnesses of 'the woman's multiple orgasms, the timing of orgasm with an airplane sound, and the acting out of fantasy'. And the moral of the video is: 'Sex just keeps getting better as we get older; the woman's initiatory capacity matches the man's.'

Or, as Keats said of Autumn:

> Where are the songs of Spring? Ay, where are they?
> Think not of them, thou hast thy music, too.

11

Problems and Answers

'Are nocturnal emissions more dangerous in married than in single men? Is masturbation a criminal offence punishable with imprisonment? My organ appears to be undersized. Are there any remedies? What diseases cause impotence? I have been told that intercourse with a young and virgin girl restores one's sexual powers when they have declined through age – is this true? Is it possible for a woman to have sex forced upon her while she is asleep? Can unorthodox methods of intercourse lead to the birth of monsters?'

Yes, sex can be a puzzling business. The kindest that can be said of George Ryley Scott, Fellow of the Zoological Society, is that he does his honest best with these and other inquiries in *Your Sex Questions Answered* (1947). There have always been those who have found difficulties with the practice as well as the theory – so much so in recent years that, according to *The Complete Book of Love and Sex*, it is now 'fashionable . . . to talk about people's sexual problems as if we were being afflicted by a new epidemic.'

The authors allow that there is something in this: 'To some extent we may be in the throes of a period of more prevalent sexual dysfunctioning, but on the other hand, because of the publicity sexual problems now receive, people who in the past would have kept quiet about them now feel willing to discuss them or seek help.'

Perversely enough, for an activity that so intimately involves the union of two sexes, any difficulties that do exist are usually discussed in books as being the particular preserve of one sex or the other. Thus males have impotence and premature ejaculation to themselves and females suffer from vaginismus or problems with orgasms, as though the one could have no possible influence on the other. But since that is the way it is done, that is the way we shall do it.

Men are allowed two main respectable difficulties – impotence and premature ejaculation: anything else is generally shunted off to 'The Byways of Sex' chapter at the back of the book. Impotence was, for some time, considered the more serious of the two complaints since it was thought to be the symptom of something really quite serious. Sperry kicks off with a fundamental variety of impotence: 'Absence of penis, whether congenital or the result of disease or accident, renders one impotent.' Fortunately this is but rarely found. A more common cause of impotency is, according to Sperry, 'sexual excess, resulting in the collapse of the nervous mechanism of the reproductive system'. Sterility, frequently confused in the minds of writers, could result from self-abuse, excess, narcotism, accident or disease. Ryley Scott agrees nearly half a century later that the sexual organs wear out with continuous use: 'There is little doubt that the abuse of the sexual powers – especially in early manhood – leads to early decay.'

Just as worrying is Havil's diagnosis of impotence in males: 'The impotent man is a man who has an insufficiency of hormones. He can often be made potent again by injections of extracts from the glands of animals which contain the necessary hormones.' But Havil, too, seems to blur the distinction between impotence and sterility. Hutton takes a less serious view, thinking the former something that tends to affect husbands early on in marriage. The husband should 'refrain from sexual stimulation or intercourse for a week or more, and then approach his wife in full confidence, and without any fear or doubting of his powers. He will find, as a rule that there is complete recovery.'

But by 1976 Tim and Beverly LaHaye are citing research showing that impotence is increasing at an alarming rate due, they say, to increasing pressure on people's sex lives. The position seems not to have improved by 1980, when Gochros and Fisher explore the subject: 'Now that the smoke has begun to clear from the revolution in female sexuality we are beginning to see that the sexual fulfilment of men has . . . been impaired by common misinformation and by the distorted expectations of male sexual behaviour.' By 1983 alarm is still more intense, with the *Complete Book of Love and Sex*'s own diagnosis: 'Public awareness and the pressure of the woman's movement over the last 20 years has definitely and provably increased men's anxieties about sexual performance, and many are now so concerned about their ability to give their partners an orgasm that they have impaired their ability to enjoy their own lives. The assertiveness of women outside the bedroom has also adversely affected many men, and this is reflected in their reduced practical interest in sex.'

Or is it simply boredom? Gochros and Fisher wonder so in their chapter, 'Problems with erections'. They suggest some by now familiar measures to inject a little interest into things: repairing to a motel room for the night, reading 'dirty' books or watching X-rated movies. The recommendations somewhat riskily go so far as to suggest 'heavy petting in a movie theatre or in a bus' ('I was only following instructions, Your Honour'). Look at Felix and Miriam, for example! They apparently overcame the tedium when they glimpsed one another in briefs and panties, one presumes respectively. The authors even recommend a rival – have a go at a few ideas from *The Joy of Sex*, they urge. 'Trying one or more of them doesn't have to be overplanned to the point of being mechanical. You don't need a big production; it can be something spontaneous that just comes over you when you're with your partner.'

Brown and Faulder deploy their own set of life class examples in order to subdivide impotence into a number of varieties. With John of Dorothy and John it is a case of 'simple impotence' brought on by mid-life work stress; Arthur of Arthur and Mavis has 'primary impotence' – i.e. there is no successful penetration; Bill of Bill and Sue has anapriapism – his erection disappears at the moment of insertion.

But Rennie MacAndrew thinks it is often no more than 'a feeling of organ inferiority'. He is rather against the 'common cure' of seeking reassurance with a prostitute. 'Recovery will need all his "intestinal fortitude", which is an American expression for the simple Anglo-Saxon "guts".' Alex Comfort thinks that all men are impotent sometimes, and that it is rarely due to physical causes and mostly due to apprehension about sexual performance.

The favourite remedies for impotence/s we will examine elsewhere. Meanwhile, we can be getting on with premature ejaculation. Ryley Scott supposes it to be simply a matter of confidence: 'If confidence in the ability to prolong the sex act can be restored, the victim is well on the way to overcoming the affliction.' MacAndrew mentions some authorities who recommend counting sheep. Chesser quotes Dr William R. Houston, who suggests 'reciting the multiplication table and remaining quite still while the female conjoint is active in securing her own orgasm'. Chesser adds drily: 'Needless to say, he should not perform this feat of memory *aloud*.'

Both MacAndrew and Parkinson-Smith advise not thinking about sex between times ('eliminate thoughts of venery'). MacAndrew urges the wife to do her bit by not undressing too quickly, 'but expose small portions of her body at a time until she is undressed, as this gives the sensitive husband's male organ time to condition itself for the part to be played'. Parkinson-Smith agrees, also tipping the occasional bathing of the genitals in cold water.

Further and better particulars of cures and exercises will follow, but let us meanwhile turn to women, noting in passing a survey cited by Exner which found that, of eighty-one vicar's wives questioned by Robert Latou Dickinson, no fewer than fifty-four suffered from some form of sexual maladjustment. An awkward statistic for Tim and Beverly.

MacAndrew adopts a robust approach to any difficulties women imagined they might have with sex. He finds numerous fears prevalent amongst the female population, and thinks probably more than 50 per cent of educated women in Britain suffer from 'some degree of coldness'. He duly embarks on a lengthy classification of these fears. There is, for example, what he calls the 'I'm too tired' or 'I'm not feeling well' variety of wife. 'Except in rare cases this is a conscious or subconscious excuse to cover up some fear or other . . . Intercourse should not tire a woman; she can participate quite passively if she wishes.' Then, more commonly, there is the wife 'who having seen the male organ thinks it much too large for her, thus setting up fear which dams up the natural processes so necessary to happy love'. There are women who fear kissing, women who consider all sex childish, women who fear pregnancy, women who claim to have had a great sexual fright in youth ('nearly everyone has had at least one bad fright. The way to get over this kind of fright is to accept it for what it is'). Then again there are women suffering from 'castration complexes' arising out of a subconscious wish that they had been men. Husbands had some responsibility in 'curing' such women. 'With the "I'll-keep-you-in-your-place" type of woman a word of warning is more useful than sympathy.'

MacAndrew certainly has little sympathy with what he terms the 'rape or seduction complex' he thinks to be prevalent among women. This, he thinks, is chiefly due to the cunning design of women's bodies which makes rape virtually impossible: 'Owing to her anatomical construction a normal woman can scarcely be forced against her will. When the male holds down her hands she can cross her legs, turn on one side, and so forth.'

Uncle Rennie offers his readers a glimpse inside the mind of the average woman involved in a so-called rape case. The scenario runs as follows: 'A girl meets a man of whom she knows little; she thinks she can take care of herself, so "for fun" goes out with him before learning anything about his character or even knowing where he lives. He probably wines and dines her well before choosing a quiet spot where he attempts to make advances.

'Possibly she cooperates a little at first just to be daring, then he tries to go too far. In the ensuing struggle the girl is more or less exhausted, but her mind is not. Let us enter her mind for a few seconds. This is something like what we'd find:

' "Good gracious! The brute! I won't let him. I'll fight (she does). Oh! he is strong. I can hardly move. What shall I do? It's useless to scream. No one will hear. No, I won't. It's not my *fault*. If I let him, I'll see what it's like. No one could blame me! A baby! No! I mustn't! Well, probably this once I wouldn't have a baby. Anyway, it's his fault. I'll see what it's like." '

Rennie's nice and old-fashioned like that. Girls still said No but meant Yes. And then what happens? 'They part company. She goes home to tell. The tale of woe is spread that the girl was assaulted. Much sympathy is wasted by her relatives and friends when in truth she deserves little.' MacAndrew sweeps to a conclusion of daring logic: 'Lady doctors, married women, school mistresses and professional women go about alone, but one scarcely ever hears of their being assaulted.'

Chesser breaks inorgasmic women down into three sorts:

1. Those who seem quite unconcerned about sexual relations, whose minds are entirely occupied with domestic duties and the like ... they regard intercourse as a duty – their obligation to their husbands, to be patiently borne.
2. The neurotic type. They often like kisses and caresses but dislike the final act. But in spite of this, they are often concerned lest their dislike of coitus should imperil their marriage.
3. Women of a warm and affectionate type ... They feel that sexual relations are not what they should be. They feel cheated. They seem vaguely to be groping for experience which will compensate for what they feel they are missing.

Chesser is not wholly sympathetic. 'These possible complexes have enjoyed far too much publicity. Today, many people – particularly women – regard it as fashionable to have a complex. Only rank outsiders lack such a valuable topic of conversation. See the look of utter astonishment which often greets a denial that one has a complex! "My dear – you simply *must* be joking!" But the plain if unexciting – truth is that people who are happy do not develop complexes. It is those who feel irritated, discontented, who suffer in this way.'

Chesser at least attributes most of the problems of the third group to faulty technique in their husbands and considers vaginismus – the tightening of the walls of the vagina so as to make intercourse impossible – 'part of the price some women have to pay for their husbands' brutal mismanagement of the sex act'. Oakley agrees that 'more females suffer from their husbands' lust-greed than from their own frigidity'. Though, incongruously enough, a couple of paragraphs later he is dictating that: 'Attack and submission are the only mechanics of the matter. The mode of attack, the manner of submission are the private affairs of the man and wife.'

Once more we are offered the life and times of handfuls of couples who won through in the end. Brown and Faulder offer us Jane of Jack and Jane ('situational loss of arousal'); Denise of Alan and Denise, who is inorgasmic; and Sally of Sally and David, who suffered from selective response. Gochros and Fisher parade Rita (painful intercourse) and Oscar; Myrna (difficulty in reaching orgasm) and Norm; Gail (didn't like sex) and Dale – as well as a sprinkling of other cases who perhaps do not fall quite as naturally into this chapter's ambit. Such as Bill (preferred love in the dark) and Linda (wanted lights left on); Annette (husband wanted her to wear garter belts and stockings); or Larry (wanted anal inter-course) and Kathy (thought Larry was sick). For help for these and other problems read on.

You want to improve your sex life? It will take you time. If you were by any chance planning to embark on all the exercises in this chapter it would be as well to clear your diary for, say, eighteen months. You will need pens, paper, notebooks, and probably a tape-recorder and vibrator. But above all you will need time. You want to become orgasmic, the Heiman/Lopiccolo way? Well, plan on nine weeks for Chapters 2 to 7; and three weeks for Chapters 8 to 10. Aim to have three individual sessions a week. Say, forty-five hours in all.

Shall we begin with a contract? Draw one up with your partner setting out your goals, the time scale and – at the end – the reward. You can find a General Purpose Contract Form on page 158 of *Treat Yourself to a Better Sex Life* by Harvey Gochros and Joel Fisher. Harvey and Joel have given us a model for a first-step contract, as drawn up by Dave and Molly:

'We agree not to engage in any mutual sexual activity for the next seven days. During that period Dave will practise relaxation exercises, using the method of deep muscle relaxation. Dave will do this every night from 8.00 to 8.30 in the family room. During this time, Molly agrees not to let the kids bother Dave. Molly agrees to let Dave know if she plans to masturbate, and Dave agrees to encourage her to do this. At the end of the week, we agree to go out to Michel's (a restaurant) as a special reward.'

You have the idea. But do not rush things. Some situational assessment is in order, in which we draw up our sexual histories. Give yourself time. The *SAR* Experience Survey runs to eight pages and sixty-three questions. 'On the average, how many different people do you presently date? What is your present dating status? How old were you at the time of your first partner-sexual experience? During your most active 24 hours how many different partners did you have? How many different sex partners have you had during your life up to now? A rough estimate will do. How many times, if ever, have you had sexual interaction with a prostitute? Ever been raped? Ever raped anyone? Ever let an animal give you sexual pleasure?'

Gochros and Fisher have their own range of questions. Answer them in a notebook or record them all on tape. There are about 160 in all, subdivided into: Pinpointing the nature and history of your problem; Any other problems? What about your good points? Early sexual experiences? Estimated frequency of activity (score from 1–5); Frequency you and your partner would prefer (ditto); Enjoyment of activities (ditto); Your feelings about your body and your appearance; Your feelings toward your present partner; Your feelings about your fantasies. Past sexual encounters that didn't turn out so well? Whom with? 'Come on, there must have been some.' No? Well, 'try to imagine some really bad ones.' Don't wilt! There is a fun exercise at the end involving completing a sentence, cereal packet-style:

I wish I could _____

I love it when _____

I get embarrassed when _____

I wish I didn't _____

I'm terrified of _____

Why not dinner at Michel's for the best entry? Only you can judge whether or not your partner is up to reading, or listening to, your answers. Lonnie Garfield Barbach (*For Yourself, The Fulfillment of Female Sexuality*, 1975) thinks there are 'some advantages to discussing your sexual history with a good male friend, or lover . . . Doing it can make the relationship closer and more intimate.' Gochros and Fisher consider such behaviour a fad from yesteryear (the sixties), 'a moving bit of philosophy, but one that probably did more harm than good'. Pragmatic Nowinski compromises: why not discuss with your partner how she would feel if you shared your past histories? If you're ready to take the risk, then carry on. But it *will* take time: 'This exercise will take at least two hours, and probably longer. You may not be able to complete it in one sitting and may need to break it up into a series of sessions. You may also want to spread these sessions over a period of time, say a month or two.'

The suggested Nowinski situational assessment stretches to forty-three questions but is, you understand, only partial. Start with childhood, work through adolescence and progress to adulthood. We're in the business of pitching 'sexual scripts' against 'sexual schemas'. Fill in the Physical Schema chart of things you find attractive and unattractive (big breasts/thick ankles/curvy calves?) and then the Character Schema Chart ('If you think you are attracted to women who like to have parties and dance, write that down as 3 in the Attractive column.')

But already we are rushing ahead. Gochros and Fisher are worrying if we even know what words to use in talking about all this, and they are not alone. The *SAR* team are bugged about the way 'dirty words' have a 'negative charge' and want to 'desensitize' or 'demythologize' them so people can use them in a casual and non-judgemental way. 'This', they explain, 'is what is meant by the idea expressed in the National Sex Forum Assumptions that people have a right to a "realistic objectification of the range of behaviour." ' You can make a start by underlining every other word or phrase in the following:

FRUITCURVEOFFLANKTOFANNYLARGELIPSNECKEYESLARGE
YESBLUEEYESEARSBREASTSBIGTITSLARGEBREASTSBARE
LEGSBARELEGSSINHEELSSLIMLEGSTHIGHSBLACKHOSE
ANKLEBRACELETFEETSTARTOFANERECTIONHARDPENIS
TIGHTFITTINGPANTSBUMPSINPANTSHAIRLONGHAIROR
LONGBLONDEPETITEFEATURESBEAUTIFULCOMPLEXION
SKINNYDIPPING

andsoforthandsoforthandsoforth. Or else you can try drawing a line between all the words that mean the same:

straight	slang	peter	hard-on
prick	cunt	redhead	boobs
lovelips	anus	penis	slit
vagina	lingam	knockers	breast
pussy	nuzzle	testicle	schmuck
clitoris	ball	orgasm	shot his wad
raincoat	coitus	stick	petting
screwing	come	cock	little man in the boat

andsoforthandsoforth. Brown and Faulder want you to set aside an hour to make two lists – one of 'expert words' and one of 'our words'. Read the list out aloud together with your partner. Then get pencil and paper and make three columns: in the third column fill in other words you know of. But, before you start, 'decide on a small prize for the one who gets the most, or a miss like making some coffee'. Then swap your pieces of paper and read your partner's words out loud. 'Now collect your prize.' Or put the coffee on.

Gochros and Fisher add a further step to the above – practising the desensitized words with your partner . . . 'Repeat them several times. Then put them in sentences, such as "I like to hold your boobs while we're screwing" or "I get real juicy while I'm stroking your cock." ' More coffee?

Now we can begin to work on opening up modes of communication. Gochros/Fisher propose some ground rules in their chapter, 'Let's Talk About Talking'. Try this seven-point plan:

1. Set aside approximately one half hour, no more than once a day, to talk about the topics we will suggest.

2. Flip a coin and decide who will be the 'first speaker'.

3. The first speaker chooses one of the topics suggested in the following exercises and tells the other person how he or she feels about the topic . . . concentrate on 'I' comments . . . statements that begin 'I wish', 'I feel' . . .

4. While the first speaker is talking the other person should listen attentively, but should not interrupt for any reason . . .

5. After the first speaker completes his or her statement the second speaker then summarizes what he or she heard the first speaker say . . . wait until the feedback is completed before you react to its accuracy, pointing out any significant omissions or alterations.

6. Now the second speaker has his or her turn to speak for five minutes. He or she can either react to the first speaker's comments or introduce another topic from the following exercises . . . again the first speaker should try to repeat what the second speaker has said.

7. Continue taking turns for up to half an hour. After you're through take a few minutes to discuss each exercise and decide on any modifications of the ground rules you both agree on. You may, for example, agree to put off responding to each other's presentations until the next session, so that you will each have time to think it over.

No, it's not terribly spontaneous, but then no one's claiming it is. After all, say Gochros/Fisher, 'we learn to walk, to talk, to drive a car – and to make love. We can't do any of these totally spontaneously – we learn them best from partners.' Ahem, and books.

So what to talk about, now you've talked about talking? The first topic in the Gochros/Fisher groundplan is to discuss your feelings about talking about sex with your partner. How uncomfortable do you feel right now about talking over your sexual relationship with your partner? How do you feel about previous attempts at discussing sex, both with your partner and with other people in the past? You can review your sexual relationship – share ideas about how to improve your own behaviour in bed. Take turns to ask the following questions: 'What aren't you getting that you would like? Are there things you wish your partner would do more often or in a different way, positions, timing, etc.? Listen to your partner's requests. Let him/her know whether the requests make sense to you.' If you run into an impasse you can move into the negotiating mode. But, wait, we're rushing ahead again. These things take time.

More on a level with the stage we've reached is the Nowinski Behavioural Reversal scheme in which we learn to communicate with an imaginary woman on the basis that when you eventually try saying them to a real woman it might be a little easier. So, imagine you're in a restaurant with a first date. Try saying out loud: 'I find you very attractive. I enjoy being with you.' Repeat it. Change the words around.

It's later. You're back in your apartment. Say 'I feel fine. But you look as if you don't.' Now say: 'I am very attracted to you, but to be honest I just don't feel ready for a sexual relationship with you yet. I'd really like to see you again and to get to know you better. I hope you can understand that.'

She understands. You've dated her again and you end up in bed making love, with you in the dominant role. Say 'Does that feel good? I'd really like it if you would tell me what feels good when I'm touching you.' Hold on a minute. All of a sudden she's asking you to do something to her which you don't fancy doing. Go on. Say: 'I'm sorry, but I really don't want to do that. Is there something else I can do for you instead?'

But this may be rushing things. Rewind the film so you're on your living-room couch again saying: 'I think you're very attractive' (if saying that makes you feel tense they suggest repeating it out loud before proceeding). She's returned the compliment. You say: 'Thank you. I'm really glad to hear that you like me, too. I really am attracted to you, but to tell you the truth, I'm feeling sort of nervous right now. If you're up to listening, I think I'd like to tell you about it.' (She is up to listening.) 'Well, the problem is I've had some sexual difficulties in the past, and it's made me sort of scared to get sexually involved . . .' That's better. Have some more coffee.

A reminder, if you are following the *SAR* Course, to fill in your journal and start reading ahead for the next session. It is time to look at ourselves and consider our body imagery. Do not rush. 'Your schedule may be busy, but you owe yourself the time,' says Nowinski. 'This is important learning you are doing here.' *SAR* people will begin with an hour in the shower or bath before moving to the full-length mirror. Brown/Faulder want you to set aside an hour in all. Don't worry about any peculiarities: Try the Brown/Faulder analogy: 'If a man selling a Volvo car spent all his time explaining to this prospective buyer why it was not a Rolls Royce, he would be doing the manufacturers, his customers and himself no good.' Some of us Renault Fours would be happy with a Volvo, but no matter, for it is time to return to the mirror with your partner. Take it in turns, ten minutes each, saying whatever comes into your head. Be frank. For example, if you consider that your partner has a fat and lumpy behind, say: 'I find your behind is fat and lumpy.'

Women may now wish to proceed to the *SAR* Sexological Exam video tape or simply accompany Lonnie Barbach on her session with hand mirror. Allow half an hour for this – 'until you have examined all the structures carefully . . . label the parts using the illustration in the Appendix.' Heiman/Lopiccolo suggest describing the structures, thinking of positive images, perhaps drawn from flowers. Write it down. You may wish, with your partner, to examine each other. The *SAR* Guide wants you to limit each exam session to thirty minutes: 'If you feel like having sex when you have finished your exam, wait until at least four hours so that you can better allow yourself to focus on the education aspects.'

But most of us are not ready even for educational intercourse. What we do next depends on whether we have a problem or not, or whether we are one of those who fall into the Brown/Faulder category of 'Sex is marvellous. Can we make it even better?' If one technique sounds very much like another this will be because it generally *is* very much like another. Sexology is not a big world. Lonnie Barbach, of the Human Sexuality Program, University of California Medical Centre, thanks no fewer than three of the authors of the *SAR* Guide, all based at the same place in the introduction to her book. Gochros and Fisher acknowledge having drawn on the work of Lonnie Barbach and Joseph Lopiccolo, one of the authors of *Becoming Orgasmic*, who are all associated with the State University of NY at Stony Brook, where Joseph Nowinski was based before going to be Director of – yes, the Human Sexuality Program at the University of California. He in turn offers thanks to Leslie Lopiccolo, another author of *Becoming Orgasmic*, and had his manuscript read by Gochros and Fisher. The British Brown and Faulder merely pay tribute to Masters and Johnson.

But then they all do this, since it was M&J who developed most of the therapeutic techniques embroidered ever since.

The common factor in most of the techniques is avoidance of intercourse for several weeks while masturbating, alone and/or with a partner, as outlined in Chapter 4, with progress via a regulated succession of exercises ('Sexpieces' in Brown/Faulder) over weeks, even months. About this stage we reach the 'Erotic Pleasure Contract' in Gochros/Fisher. The contracts are for providing clarity. You should each have a copy. 'If you do use an oral agreement, we suggest that it be limited to an initial agreement — say, to read this book and discuss it until a formal plan and specific goals can be agreed upon. Then these goals should be put in writing.' 'Remember,' add Gochros/Fisher, 'they can be renegotiated if they turn out to be unsatisfactory.' A ten-point guideline is set out for preliminary negotiations over what should go into the contract, much of which could be fruitfully adapted for use in the industrial scene — 4, for example: 'Compromise. Be prepared to give a little. This might mean having a "fall-back" position if you run into trouble with your negotiations.'

But back to the Erotic Pleasure Contract, for which we once again have a welcome model to guide us:

'Morton and Jill agree to practise Erotic Pleasure 2 for a period of up to ten days. We will do this for a period of one hour, in bed, at night (after 10 o'clock). We agree to follow the exact steps as outlined in *Treat Yourself to a Better Sex Life*. However, if either of us dislikes one of these steps, we will not use it, and the other partner promises not to put down the one who dislikes the step. We will practise the technique until Morton can maintain an erection for at least fifteen minutes straight, and then for three sessions in a row. We will have sessions at least every Monday, Wednesday and Friday. We also agree to sleep in the nude and to hold each other for at least fifteen minutes before going to sleep. We will not attempt to engage in sexual intercourse during this period.' Alas, no reward is stipulated. Perhaps they could join up with Dave and Molly at Michel's?

On we soldier. Exercises in 'informational massage', 'unlearning sexual negativity' and orgasmic role-playing ('use new words, growls, moans, whispers, panting, screaming, laughing') and other sound-exploration ('such as bed-squeaking, fingers squishing,

PROBLEMS AND ANSWERS

sheets rustling, air wooshing in and out of your vagina') with *SAR*.
With Brown/Faulder we listen to each other's stomachs gurgling.
With Heiman/Lopiccolo we have more role-playing orgasm
('moan, scratch, pummel the bed, cry – the more exaggerated the
better') and vibrator technique: 'try to compare a few different
models. Do they feel comfortable to hold, and do they fit on your
hand well? How does the weight feel?' Best Buy: the over-hand
Oster, or the hand-held Prelude, which, encouragingly, also comes
well out of the Gochros/Fisher trials.

Gochros/Fisher advise working out a distress signal before
indulging in some of the more advanced exercises: 'It can be
anything you want – a tap on the hand or a brief statement ("This
is uncomfortable"). Whatever you choose, both of you should
agree in advance as to what the signal is, you should offer it as soon
as you begin to feel uncomfortable, and you should try to do it
without hostility or without putting your partner down ("I said,
'Cut it Out, Stupid' ").'

Get in touch with your body, get your needs out on the table,
exercise those sex muscles, work out with fantasy, fill in your stress
chart to establish tension ratings, master the Herbert Benson
relaxation method, let yourself be sexual, develop your sexuality
further ('this process takes time and persistence, as well as a good
measure of patience.') Fill in your Caring Behaviors List; and now
your Pleasant Activities List. Set aside an hour to talk about
sharing and intimacy . . . pretty soon we'll be approaching non-
demand intercourse.

Meanwhile, those with erection problems will be on exercise 8 of
Nowinski, filling in their Erection Dysfunction Questionnaire, and
those with genital phobias will be on exercise 7 – Letting Yourself
Look. Buy several soft-porn mags such as *Playboy* and spend five
minutes a day shifting your attention back and forth among the
different parts of their bodies, including the genitals. 'If and when
you begin to have any negative reactions (tension, disgust) shift
your attention to another part of the body for a moment.'
Premature ejaculators will be on Chapter 10; retarded ejaculators
will concentrate on Chapter 12.

All these things are your *right*. 'Everyone has a right to a good
sex life,' the *SAR* Guide insists. 'You have a right', say Gochros/
Fisher, 'to establish conditions for having sex the way you want it.'
'Remember,' Nowinski prompts you, 'you have the right to decline

152

to do things that are not to your own tastes.' Do you feel ready now? Then negotiate an all-the-way contract like Jon and Marge's:

'Jon and Marge agree to attempt intercourse beginning on Sunday. Marge will masturbate Jon until he has a firm erection. Then, Marge will' . . . andsoforthandsoforth . . . 'We will try this for three nights in a row, in bed, and at the usual time of our session. If we are successful for three nights in a row, we will treat ourselves to a movie and dinner. Also, after three straight days of success, we will set up a new contract so that both of us can achieve orgasm during intercourse.'

A movie *and* dinner! Well, you've earned it. Those who did not quite stay the course will find a helpful section at the back of Gochros/Fisher on 'Choosing a Therapist'. Those who did may care to venture further with Nowinski in Expanding Your Sexual Repertoire: 'You'll need about an hour, plus two pencils or pens in different colours. The instructions assume that you will be using blue and red although, of course, you may substitute others. You will also need the Sexual Activity Checklist and the Sexual Activity Coding Sheet. The exercise is to be done in two parts. Go through the Sexual Activity Checklist slowly and carefully. Note that each activity listed has a number and that these numbers appear on the Sexual Activity Coding Sheet as well. There are a total of 33 specific sexual activities . . . For each activity listed, indicate a *pleasure rating* on the Sexual Activity Coding Sheet. (Do this in red.)' Andsoforthandsoforth. It is all your right. But winning rights always did take time.

12

Harps and Harpies

The working-class wife is comforting the young bride whose husband has just gone off to the front in the Great War. 'No, my dear, you don't know what you're up agen yet. But wait until you've been to bed over 3,000 nights with the same man like me and had to put up with everything. Then you'd be blooming glad the old Kayser went potty.'

Two strands of patriotism – one fighting for England, another thinking of it – and how gratefully we recognize, in the older woman, the very type of the headache-prone, middle-aged wife who once a week for thirty years reluctantly consents to submit to her husband's marital rights and rites. The scene is from a book by Margaret Eyles, published in 1922 and quoted in *The Cost of English Morals* (1931) by Janet Chance, a feminist who spent her Tuesdays helping to run a sex education and advice centre in Bow Road, East London.

Tuesdays rather lead her to agree with the anti-type Margaret Eyles presents. Of ninety-three women who call in for advice twenty-nine specifically complain that they have never, or only rarely, experienced sexual satisfaction – indeed, the response at East End working women's meetings is that it is 'often new to women that they might at all share the sex enjoyment of their husbands . . . Some women do not know whether they know [passion] or not!

'Passion in England remains a lopsided affair. The men, more or less, know what can be. The women, for their part, often do not,' concludes Janet Chance, who thinks that 'it is probably true of not less than half the marriages of today in England, possibly of many more, that the wife habitually experiences the passion of another in the absence of her own . . . Too often the moment which for the man is the culmination of ecstasy and romance is for the woman an intimate, too intimate, assistance at a distasteful business . . . Such women have often lain awake, saying to themselves that marriage is the real prostitution because in it something finer than the hopes of a prostitute is continually destroyed.'

However it was diminished in practice, and contrary to popular maxim, there was early acknowledgement that most women were possessed of a libido. One has to go right back to William Acton, writing in 1857 (*The Functions and Disorders of the Reproductive Organs, in Childhood, Youth, Adult Age, and Advanced Life, Considered in their Physiological, Social and Moral Relations*) to find the generally-credited originator of the concept of universal 'sexual anaesthesia' (to use van de Velde's happy phrase) in women. But by 1884 Elizabeth Blackwell is stating as a 'well-established fact that in healthy loving women, uninjured by the too-frequent lesions which result from childbirth, increasing physical satisfaction attaches to the ultimate physical expression of love' and dismissing 'the prevalent fallacy that sexual passion is the almost exclusive attribute of men'.

This desire in women, while acknowledged, is widely felt to be something that hibernates, to surface only when fortuitously unlocked by a man. Norval Geldenhuys thinks that, at the time of marrying, man's emotions are 'much more intense, much more eager to be satisfied, and consequently much stormier' but that 'woman's sexual passions have been more or less dormant'. Isabel Hutton (1953) agrees that long before marriage 'the man has been quite aware of his sexual instinct and has had a specially strong attraction towards his wife. She on the other hand, may never have experienced sex emotion for the man she marries.' In George Ryley Scott's view (1947), the desires are not so much dormant as caged, awaiting man's merciful release. Just see what happens to a woman who goes through life without the key ever turning in the lock: 'Sex is a biological need in a woman's life as it is in a man's. It is a fact so noteworthy as to rank almost as a platitude that the middle-aged spinster is unhappy, bad-tempered and so psychologically abnormal that she is difficult to live with . . . the reason for the evolution of this type of mind is sex repression.'

Chesser fears for women tempted to experiment with sex before marriage, little anticipating the tidal wave unleashed by their first sexual experience: 'Another myth which has grown up in recent years is that a woman who sows her "wild oats" before marriage is no more affected than are the innumerable men who have indulged in sexual relationships prior to wedlock. I accept the contention that woman's sexuality is comparable to man's so far as its strength is concerned. But its nature is different. The woman does not play precisely the same role as the man in a sex relationship. She may engage in the sex act with as much ardour as her partner. But if this act is outside of the fuller relationship which is so necessary to her well-being, both on social grounds and because of her feminine sexual nature, she will be giving away something which means much more to her than anything the man gives.

'Almost invariably, the woman who indulges in sexual intercourse experiences thereafter a greatly heightened desire for further congress. Very often there arises an insatiable desire to repeat the experience. This accounts for the astonishing manner in which highly intelligent, charming women sometimes give themselves to thoroughly degraded men. They simply cannot help themselves. Starting out in search of "sex equality", they end by becoming the slaves of their emotional selves.' And, hence, of men.

Chesser does not believe women to be wholly oblivious to the sexual urge during adolescence, but insists that 'in the overwhelming majority of cases, it has to be "brought out" by suitable action on a lover's part'. He believes women incapable of viewing intercourse as a single copulatory act, but rather as part of a series embracing 'courtship, wooing, sex act, conception, gestation, childbirth, lactation and maternity'.

This view of woman's nature permeates most of the advice contained in books on sex for decades on end. Woman awaits you men! It is all up to you. Play up, Play up, and play the Game! Most of the resultant books are by men, for men. Men, men assume, are more interested and more experienced in sex. Men, men assume, initiate sex while women respond. And women *will* respond to those suitably tutored in the art of sex. Which, since you mention it, is why you need this book. That will be three and sixpence please.

The vanity that shoulders all the responsibility for all woman's pleasure is quite broad-shouldered enough to accept the blame for woman's failure to achieve satisfaction, so that there is no great reticence in acknowledging the sort of situation described by Janet Chance. It is easy enough to explain. As far back as 1859 Jules Guyot, in his little book reissued in 1931, attributes women's unhappy experience of sex to precisely such untutored men: 'There exists no woman without sex needs, there exists no woman without desire, there exists none incapable of the sex orgasm. But on the other hand, unfortunately, there exists an immense number of masculine ignoramuses, egotists, brutes, who do not take pains to study the musical instrument God has confided to them.' Women had no option but to take consolation in sacrifice and resignation when left unsatisfied 'through the ignorance or the indolence or the egotism of the man; when, above all, the wife passes her entire married life under the influence of perpetual stimulation without her sex function ever being complete and normal, the depression, the fatigue, the disgust, and often a despair whose causes are unknown to her, overwhelm her life and bring in their train maladies which resist all healing treatment'.

Thompson, in 1917, is also forthright in condemning 'a man's passion for possession [which] leads him to adopt hustling methods in his lovemaking, a sudden insistent demand that there shall be no beating about the bush'. To a woman, 'although her desire to possess may be as great, there is a joy in more leisurely courtship'. Similarly, Marie Stopes complains of the way in which man 'approaches [woman] or not as is his will. Some of her rhythms defy him – the moon-month tide of menstruation, the cycle of ten moon-months of bearing the growing child . . . but the subtler ebb and flow of woman's sex has escaped man's observation or his care . . . In our anaemic artificial days it often happens that the man's desire is a surface need, quickly satisfied, colourless, and lacking beauty, and that he has no knowledge of the rich complexities of love-making which an initiate of love's mysteries enjoys.'

An alternative line, for those reluctant to criticize men – even those of little learning – is that taken by Sperry in 1900, in which he blames the hypocrisy of society for the existence of a 'few women to whom the act is always positively distasteful – not to say disgusting'. He bemoans the fact that 'so many women think it derogatory and shameful to admit the possession of sexual passion. Not a few women think it a cause for congratulation that they have a positive distaste for all sexual activity, and they are quite apt, on occasion, to impress their views on others. Those who have strong passions are quite as apt to keep silence respecting themselves, for fear of ridicule or censure from their cold-blooded sisters.'

Sperry's study of the subject leads him to believe there are three categories of women:

1. (The smallest group.) Those who are naturally as amorous and as responsive in sexual passion as the average man;
2. (The largest group.) Those who, while less passionate than men, still have positive desire for, and take actual pleasure in, sexual congress – especially just preceding menstruation and immediately following its periodical cessation.
3. Those who experience no physical passion or pleasurable sexual sensations and submit to copulation only from a sense of duty, or for the purpose of bearing children, or simply for the pleasure of gratifying the husband.

But whatever the category of woman, they are all to be considered as a challenge. Or, to adopt Guyot's metaphor, they are all musical instruments awaiting the virtuoso's touch. Actually, it was Balzac who said it first: 'In love, woman is a harp who only yields her secrets of melody to the master who knows how to handle her.' And so apt was Balzac's epigram considered that van de Velde repeats it, adding his own embellishment: 'But who can play this delicate human harp aright, unless he knows all her chords, and all the tones and semitones of feeling? Only the genius – after long practice and many discords and mistakes. But, in marriage, such discords are unspeakably painful. So the husband who wants to be more than the blunderer, and if his marriage is to be happy he must be more, must study the art of music.' (He adds, in all modesty: 'Till now, there was no accessible book of rules for him.') So apt, Balzac, that Helena Wright dusts the quote off for use in *The Sex Factor in Marriage* (1930), adding her own variation: 'A woman's body can be regarded as a musical instrument awaiting the hand of an artist. Clumsiness and ignorance will produce nothing but discord.' And so apt, Helena's Wright's epigram, that Norval Geldenhuys repeats it, with due acknowledgement, in 1952. A less-frequently quoted Balzac *bon mot* (though van de Velde airs it happily enough) runs: 'No man should marry before he has studied anatomy and dissected the body of a woman.'

MacAndrew daringly switches arts in 1938: 'The hardest marble in the hands of a master can be made into a beautiful statue; the coldest woman can be transformed into a warm-hearted life companion, for the cold shadows of frigidity cannot withstand the brilliance of the sun of love.'

But to return to music, and to van de Velde, the rewards are great for the instrumentalist who has truly devoted himself to the study of those scales and arpeggios, for he will find he 'may enter and enjoy the realm of free fancy according to his gifts . . . Meanwhile, the resonant harp has been itself transformed into an artist in melody, that seeks and sings, and . . . entrances the initiator.'

See how the woman changes when skilfully harmonized and orchestrated: 'It invigorates and develops the physique generally and replaces infantile outlines and proportions by those typical of maturity. This is especially the case with the bosoms . . . it develops all the latent strength and sweetness of a woman's character, ripens her judgement, gives her serenity and poise. This is not only the case in the long run, as a result of the sum of sexual acts and impressions; it is also true of each single successful occasion. Each such satisfactory erotic experience revives and refreshes the healthy woman throughout her soul and body.'

Is this not cause for true gratitude towards the harpist? MacAndrew thinks so: 'For successful married love the man must generally occupy the aggressive role, woman the submissive one . . . to be the submissive partner is truthfully woman's greatest privilege, for although she is ruled by the man, at the same time she holds him captive.' And, again, elsewhere: 'The wife who does not thrill to her husband's caress is making a mistake which may cost her dearly. A good wife must reject all girlhood inhibitions, fixations, complexes, or whatever specialists care to call them, and boldly face love, which is the central fact of life.'

Are women aware enough of the compliments the harpist pays them? Gilbert Oakley doubts it. He instructs wives how they should react should, say, their husbands, be unable to function properly unless by approaching their wives from behind: 'This', says Dr Oakley, 'is a compliment to the wife. Indeed, every sexual act performed on a woman by a man is a compliment to the woman. For it is an acceptance of her sex-appeal for him to the exclusion of other women.'

But Dr Oakley is nothing if not even-handed. He thinks 'the reasonable, *reasoning* man' should find affectionate pleasure in indulging his wife's 'little kinks' as well, since they are also a compliment to *him*. For example: 'Some wives prefer to take the active position from time to time. They like to have the man underneath and to go through the vigorous, masculine movements

until mutual orgasm is achieved.' Harpy Turns on Harpist Shock!
'If the wise husband permits this, he is not being disloyal to his sex,
demeaning himself or making himself female by playing the
feminine role. He is giving his wife the satisfaction of working off
the masculine side of her nature from time to time, in just the same
way in which *he* might like to work off the feminine side to his
nature by wearing girls' undies.' (Which, naturally, the wife
should accept, too: 'If her husband has a decent figure and is
taking care of it, he does not look unattractive in neat feminine
underwear any more than he does in masculine underwear.')

'Sex', says Dr Oakley, feeling for another metaphor, 'is like an
electric light circuit. There are positive and negative elements.' It
does not need saying that 'Man is the positive element, the
conqueror; woman the negative, the conquered'.

Tim and Beverly LaHaye (1976) have, as we would expect,
found the Biblical evidence. After repeated cautions against
nagging they warn wives against attempted dominance: 'Next to
nagging, nothing is less pleasing to a husband than a domineering
wife. There is just nothing feminine about a domineering woman.
Any woman with a problem of this kind needs to pursue a Bible
study on Ephesians 5:17–24 and 1 Peter 3:1–7, then ask God to
give her submissive grace.' Tim and Beverly give an outline of
what submissive grace might mean in the context of the bedroom
department: 'Remember,' they remind wives, 'you are a responder.
God placed within the feminine heart the amazing ability to
respond to her husband. Most women admit to having exciting
experiences they would never otherwise have attempted except in
response to something initiated by their husbands. This is
particularly true of their love lives. Except for those occasions
when a wife is particularly amorous and initiates love-making, the
husband makes the first approach most of the time.'

Tim and Beverly are, as we know, quaintly old-fashioned in
many of their views, and proud of it. Elsewhere, inch-by-inch
concessions have been made towards allowing women to escape
from the harp role. Havil, in 1939, complains that 'far too many
women just lie still, letting the husband proceed as he wishes,
meanwhile feeling terribly self-satisfied at performing their marital
duties'. Chesser, while telling readers that 'man can take the lead
in all that relates to sexual union and for the great majority that is
as it should be . . . most women want him to,' does not wish

women to suppose that they must 'invariably remain passive during congress or, if they do not, that they must be creatures of wholly exceptional sexuality. This is quite erroneous.'

Lucia Radl has an even more ambitious view of woman's role in 1953: 'Sexual compatibility in marriage is even more important to a woman than it is to a man. A woman's whole life is bound up in her sex. She has, in most cases, no other career except that of being a wife and mother. A man, on the other hand, is engrossed in his work. If his sex life is not satisfying he can pour his energies into his outside career. Not so a woman. Hence it behoves you to learn all you can about marital relations and to make certain that your love-making is thrilling and satisfying in all respects.'

Do not get carried away. This is not to deny that 'in all relations between the sexes in our society the man is the aggressor and initiator . . . but should your husband fall short in this important function (and most men do fall far short of attaining the mutual satisfaction and joy that is possible) it is up to you to improve the situation. Women's role in sex is more passive than that of the male, but it is not nearly so passive as was once thought.' It may be thought rather hard on women to be held responsible in this way for something that was largely supposed to be out of their hands, but Dr Radl does her best to explain how it may be done. She begins with a warning of how not to do it: 'Don't become bored with your husband's love. This can only lead to unhappiness and frigidity – probably to infidelity and divorce. Instead, get at the seat of the trouble and work out a better, happier relationship. Like the male, you, too, should experience a climax of orgasm at the peak of sexual union.' You *can* make love to him sometimes: 'Despite the fact that your husband is the initiator in sexual courtship, he still likes to receive as well as to give attention.'

The idea of women as harps, silently waiting to be tuned and plucked still remains, though it ultimately degenerates into blackmail. We have seen two examples already – MacAndrew warning the woman who does not thrill to her husband's caress that she is 'making a mistake which may cost her dearly'; and Oakley telling wives that every sex act is a compliment to them 'for it is an acceptance of her sex-appeal for him to the exclusion of other women'. Oakley goes even further in instructing wives to accept any transvestite tendencies in their husbands, for 'if it finds expression in the marriage bedroom, it is safer than if the husband has to seek out another partner, outside the married state, who is more understanding and more willing to cooperate'. Other writers obligingly chime in with the same theme. 'J' tells her aspiring sensuous women readers that 'married or not, men are going to continue to go looking, and a great number will sample women besides yourself. You may not like it, but you're going to have to live with it.' A few tips on keeping him reined in are contained in a section entitled 'Pleasing the Polygamist': 'It's women who keep marriage alive and benefit most from it. So get this straight. If she is going to keep her man monogamous, it's woman's responsibility to give him the sexual variety and adventure at home that he could find easily on his own elsewhere.'

'J' contrives to produce the inversion of the old-fashioned sort of sex manual, even down to the inversion of the same imagery – only by now we've graduated from the harp to the piano: 'Realize that no man is going to play the game with you very long unless you can make him feel like he is a Rubinstein on a good day. So we're going to turn you into a concert grand.'

Penitence is offered up for those liberated years (this is all of 1970) when women, 'after centuries of unexpressed hunger', feasted. 'We were so busy in bed getting "satisfied" that we forgot our responsibilities as women. We were greedy, selfish and stupid.' They have erred and strayed like lost sheep and now, says 'J', they must make atonement. 'Pin up on your bed, your mirror, your wall a sign, lady, until you *know* it in every part of your being: "We were designed to delight, excite and satisfy the male of the species." *Real* women know this.' And 'J' knows what she is going to do about it: 'I'll be darned if I'm going to, through lack of energy and imagination, encourage him to find that new experience with some sexy young thing at the office. He's a fantastic man and worth swinging from a chandelier for occasionally.'

You don't actually have to go that far. The most important thing, says Marabel Morgan (1973) is to keep looking good. Keep your eye on the competition. 'What about it, girls . . . would your husband pick you for his mistress?' Which wife who wanted to stay a wife would 'get up in the morning and serve him breakfast looking like a witch if she knew how the girls in the office look?' Think back to the time you first met your husband. Then ask yourself: 'What did you look like last night when he came home? What did you have on this morning when he left for work. Girls, is it any wonder the honeymoon is over and instead of feeling sought, you both feel caught?'

Fizzle, as Marabel Morgan puts it, to Sizzle! 'One of your husband's most basic needs is for you to be physically attractive to him . . . Many a husband rushes off to work leaving his wife slumped over a cup of coffee in her grubby undies. His once sexy bride is now wrapped in rollers and smells like bacon and eggs. All day long he's surrounded at the office by dazzling secretaries who emit clouds of perfume . . . This is all your husband asks from you. He wants the girl of his dreams to be feminine, soft and touchable when he comes home. That's his need. If you are dumpy, stringy or exhausted he's sorry he came . . . Is it any wonder so many men come home late, if at all?'

All this has echoes of Helena Wright's advice of thirty years earlier: 'Nowadays many husbands and wives work together and so see a good deal of each other in sober working moods. These wives would do well not to let their husbands forget that they also have a feminine, decorative, even "frilly" side to their natures.' For Marabel Morgan sherry time is the crucial time of day for frills. 'Remember, fellow wives, a man thinks differently than we do. Before a man can care about who a woman is he must first get past that visual barrier of how a woman looks. So your appearance at 6.00 pm should have top priority. Those first four minutes when he arrives home at night set the atmosphere for the entire evening. Greet him at the door with your hair shining, your beautifully made-up face radiant, your outfit sharp and snappy – even though you're not going anywhere. He'll feel more alive just coming home to you when your whole countenance and attitude say "Touch me. I'm yours." ' And, as for later in the evening, remember 'your husband wants a warm, comforting and eager partner. If you're stingy in bed, he'll be stingy with you. If you're available to him, you need not worry about him looking elsewhere.' Tim and Beverly LaHaye speak highly of Marabel Morgan and her sizzle/ fizzle technique: 'Clean up, paint up, fix up' is Tim and Beverly's own motto for wives to keep in mind 'just before the time of hubby's arrival'. They do not say if it's Old or New Testament.

All in all, it didn't take long for some women to trade in passive harpdom for active guilt. So sorry I didn't fizzle enough for you. Quite understand if you'd like to see if you can do better elsewhere. So long. But men, fragile violets, are having some difficulty coming

to terms with the New Woman all the same and might consider
having handy a copy of Alexandra Penney's understanding little
book, published in 1981. Ms Penney had read *The Joy of Sex*, 'J',
Love Without Fear and *More Joy of Sex*, to name but a few, and
decided that nothing had been written dealing specifically with
men's needs, so she set out to tell women *How to Make Love to a Man*.
We learn of 'The Surprising Six: Men's Biggest Sexual Fears'
(Temporary Impotence, Keeping it Up, Coming Too Soon, Am I
Gay, Ageing and Size – 'You check out other guys' dongs because
you want to know what your competition is.'); the two positions
'that help a man feel as if he's had a fireworks orgasm'; tricks of the
trade from prostitutes and call girls; dealing with erection
problems ('empathize . . . then work out a plan to take the pressure
off him'); and Setting the Scene (' "Every man I know," says
Sheila, a very seductive executive secretary, "is turned on by a
book of photographs by Helmut Newton. It's called White
Women. I keep it right on the coffee table." ') A touch overbearing
with the technique? But, says Ms Penney, 'you *must* be technically
good. Most women have never been made aware of the importance
of technique. They assume that making love is a natural
experience.' Surely not? 'This is only partially true. You *do* know
what to do instinctively, but there is a lot to be learned about what
a man likes and when, where, and how he likes it. Men feel that
women are lacking in know-how in certain areas, and they're often
too shy or embarrassed to let their wives or lovers know. Think
about how many women suffered in silence until men learned what
women needed physically and emotionally.'

More radical sisters of 'J', Marabel and Alexandra would
doubtless accuse them of having fallen into the trap of writing
books with the same agenda as the old sex manuals they sought to
replace. Read the four-point agenda set for women by the *Sexual
Attitude Restructuring Guide* for the contrast:

1. Women can have orgasm any way they prefer.
2. A woman can decide if she wants her orgasm(s) before
   intercourse, during intercourse, and/or afterwards.
3. A woman can define her own sexual lifestyle. Many women
   today find that there is a wide variety of lifestyles, one or
   more of which fit their individual needs. Some women are
   choosing long-term marriage contracts; some are choosing

'open marriages' which include outside relationships. Some relationships last a short time and some last a long time. Some women are choosing to live together with their partners; some prefer to live alone or in groups. Some relationships are monogamous. Some women don't want a primary partner at all. Some women are choosing to relate to partners of the same sex, and some women prefer to have sex with themselves exclusively. There are times when women don't want sex at all.

4. A woman can experience pleasure in sex without necessarily having an orgasm.

WE NEED SELF-KNOWLEDGE, FACTS, OPTIONS, TECHNIQUES, HONESTY.

There you have one or two options to be getting on with at least. Meanwhile the trusty old harp is comprehensively dumped by Sheila Kitzinger, who, funnily enough, came across it, not in a book, but from the lips of a man who, one imagines, was not fully au fait with all the nuances of modern feminism. 'A man once told me', Ms Kitzinger recounts, 'that making love to a woman is like playing a musical instrument and that once you know the techniques they can be applied to any woman with equal effectiveness.' Oh dear, oh dear. But Ms Kitzinger crushes him into the ground really quite courteously: 'All the evidence coming from women themselves about what is important to them in lovemaking suggests that this just is not true. Each new relationship requires its own artistry and lovers need to discover how to construct their own patterns of lovemaking and find a harmony that is right for them. It is a creative process quite different from the idea of being programmed for orgasm.'

The balance of Ms Kitzinger's own book is significant. We have sixteen pages on sexual harassment, assault and pornography; thirteen pages on loving women; nine pages of developing self-confidence in sex, including assertiveness technique; nine pages on massage; two or three pages on touching and stroking 'without being made to feel that it is always the prelude to intercourse'; two pages on clitoral stimulation; four paragraphs on oral stimulation. And, finally, two paragraphs on intercourse, beginning: 'If penetration occurs.' By no means a small 'if'.

The drift away from emphasis on intercourse inherent in this and other recent feminist writings on sex would probably not have greatly surprised Elizabeth Blackwell. She speaks of 'affectionate husbands of refined women [who] often remark that their wives do not regard the distinctively sexual act with the same intoxicating physical enjoyment that they themselves feel, and they draw the conclusion that the wife possesses no sexual passion.' Whereas 'a delicate wife will often confide to her medical adviser that at the very time when married love seems to unite them most closely, when her husband's welcome kisses and caresses seem to bring them into profound union, comes an act which mentally separates them.' It is, she says, a fallacy to regard sexual passions as being 'attached exclusively to the act of coition – a fallacy which . . . arises from ignorance of the distinctive character of human sex, viz, its powerful mental element.'

As for all the Marabel Morgan business about dressing up at six and sizzling to fizzle: 'When they have been together with a man for a few years they realize that men take far less trouble to be attractive to them,' writes Sheila Kitzinger. 'The un-deodorized, unshaven male with a grubby collar, scratchy toenails and calloused hands can be pretty revolting! Women say their partners have unpleasant habits, many of which interfere with lovemaking, such as "burping", "breaking wind", "scratching", "snorting with catarrh", smoking ("I wish he would give up smoking. I can smell the faggy smell even when he has brushed his teeth a couple of times and rinsed with mouthwash") and drinking ("If my husband has been drinking I don't like to kiss him because he has stale breath").'

Yes, after 3,000 nights of that you might well be blooming glad the Kayser went potty.

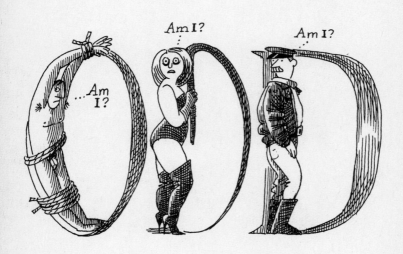

13

Am I Odd?

Most people, according to Dr Alex Comfort, have at least one 'preferred sex behaviour' which a judge would find odd. Judges had better read no further. Would that one could return to those innocent days when His Lordship could turn to members of the jury and explain in a kindly voice: 'Abnormal vice abounds on the Continent, where the virtue of Christianity has fallen into contempt' (Elizabeth Blackwell, 1884). Or else: 'There are . . . forms of secret vice that occasionally stagger and horrify ordinary healthily-minded men, but their vogue in Britain is, I believe, extremely limited' ('A Physician', 1925).

Even van de Velde, not a squeamish man, finds it difficult to face up foursquare to the subject: 'We refer exclusively to normal intercourse between opposite sexes . . . if we cannot avoid occasional references to certain abnormal sexual practices we shall emphatically state that they are abnormal. But this will only occur very seldom, for, as postulated above, it is our intention to keep the Hell-gate, or the Realm of Sexual Perversions, firmly closed.'

Dr van de Velde, perhaps you would be so good as to explain to members of the jury what you mean by 'normal'?

Van de Velde: 'That intercourse which takes place between two sexually mature individuals of opposite sexes, which excludes cruelty and the use of artificial means for producing voluptuous sensations; which aims directly or indirectly at the consummation of sexual satisfaction, and concludes with the ejaculation – or emission – of the semen into the vagina, at the nearly simultaneous culmination of sensation – or orgasm – of both partners.'

A model of judicial phrasing. Let us try out some other definitions to match against van de Velde's exacting standard. *Call Rennie MacAndrew*: 'No reasonable means of stimulation which leads up to and culminates in intercourse is a perversion, providing nothing other than the two bodies is used.' MacAndrew includes rubber bands in this. 'Of course the man who gets pleasure by beating his wife is deviating from normal, but mutual and playful little smacks could not be called abnormal.' Satisfactory, m'lud? *Call Dr Eustace Chesser.*

Dr Chesser, it has been said that anything which leads up to emission of the male semen into the vagina is normal?

Dr Chesser: 'But this is not entirely true, for many sadists practise vile cruelty, yet finally enjoy coitus with the person they have ill-treated. All sorts of perverted practices are used by some to stimulate them for final coitus.'

Call Miss Jane Cousins.

Miss Cousins: 'Whatever a couple decides to do, whatever variations they hit upon, if both enjoy doing it and find it exciting and satisfying, it's not going to harm anyone. It isn't perverted, abnormal or sick if the aim behind it is to *share* pleasure and if you know you're being careful with someone else's feelings.'

Call Dr Alex Comfort.

Dr Comfort: 'Any sex behaviour is normal which:

1. You both enjoy,
2. Hurts nobody,
3. Isn't associated with anxiety,
4. Doesn't cut down on your scope.'

Is there nothing you would consider unusual?

'Some sex behaviours are obviously odd, and restrict the range of enjoyment – like . . .'

Yes, Dr Comfort?

'Like the man who could only get orgasm by getting into a bath of cooked spaghetti. He, however, liked it that way.'

Recall Dr Eustace Chesser. Dr Chesser, it has been suggested that anything is permissible provided that one's partner enjoys it?

Dr Chesser: 'Very little consideration reveals that this will not do at all. If the partners were two thoroughly perverted people, anything could be held to be justified. In the extreme case of a sadist and masochist, even mutual murder might be held to be justified, which is clearly absurd. One must draw the line somewhere.'

Where?

'That is the question. It is one which is not easily answered. Indeed, to lay down any hard-and-fast rule is exceedingly dangerous. So much depends upon the individuals concerned and their circumstances. It is, however, worth observing that the dividing line between what is generally accepted as normal and what is clearly perverse, is an extremely thin one. Many practices can be considered perfectly normal when indulged in as a means to an end – the end being intercourse – but must be regarded as abnormal when indulged in as an end in themselves.'

Dr Lewis Smedes, you are a professor of Theology. Can you help us with a definition?

'Since there is no rule from heaven, it is likely that the only restraint is the feelings of the other person. For example, if one partner has guilt feelings about oral sex, the Christian response of the other will be to honour them until he/she adjusts his/her feelings. On the other hand if the partner has only aesthetic reservations, and if these are rooted in some fixed idea that sex is little more than a necessary evil, anyway, he/she has an obligation to be taught, tenderly and lovingly, of the joys of sex in the freedom of Christ. Any couple exploring new territories of sexual activity ought to feel free and open for discovery of new avenues of delight. The Christian word is: "Try it. If you like it, it is morally good for you." '

Does that extend to exploring homosexual 'avenues of delight'?

Prof. Smedes: 'The sexuality of every person is meant to move him toward a heterosexual union of committed love.'

Call Tim and Beverly LaHaye. Is this also your understanding of the scriptures?

Tim and Beverly: 'The Bible is very clear on homosexuality. It is an abnormal, deviant practice according to Romans 1:27. The children of Israel were commanded by God to stone to death homosexuals (Lev. 20:13), a severe treatment intended to keep them from becoming contagious. Every homosexual is potentially an evangelist of homosexuality capable of perverting many young people to his sinful way of life. Homosexuality seems to be the ultimate sin in the Bible that causes God to give men up.'

But enough of this adversarial hectoring. Let the witnesses muddle on for themselves, and let them continue with homosexuality, since that is where we appear to have reached. Unhappily, our next witness, 'A Physician' (1925) finds the task difficult, since 'secret vices are beyond the power of ordinary language'. Still, he will do his best to tell us how widespread is the problem.

'I cannot conceive of the mental condition of their votaries, and can only regard it as a form of degeneration that is closely allied to Insanity. Yet those who know the underworld of the educated and well-to-do constantly meet instances of these, and their devotees are often blatant and unconcerned about their vices. You will find in the purlieus of vice of the great cities men who paint their faces and direct the ogling glances of the harlot at other men, satyrs of the human race. In the Army, in Public Schools, in the Navy, even, instances of an offence that is punishable by two years' hard labour are constantly cropping up. Even clergymen have been found to practise this secret vice.'

Leslie Weatherhead may be more coherent in explaining its cause. 'Homosexuality is of two kinds, (1) innate and (2) acquired.

1. Innate homosexuality. This is one of the most distressing disharmonies which the psychologist will ever have to meet. There are some physical diseases which, at the present advance-point of medical and surgical science, are incurable. The inversion is thought by some to be due to remote prenatal causes.
2. Acquired homosexuality. This is a perversion practised by those who indulge in sexual relations of the same sex. It is sometimes brought on in men by sex assault and unscrupulous manipulation in childhood. It is brought on in both sexes by acquired cerebral disease by over-stimulation of the sexual centres, especially in early life.'

Weatherhead considers the most potent argument against inverted practices that the 'sex instinct is roused and yet is not satisfied'. He produces a telling metaphor: 'It is bad enough to keep a hungry man in a barn where there is neither smell nor sight of food. It is a cruel torture to take him repeatedly to a hotel grill room, within sight and smell of food and then take him back to the barn.'

The Reverend Barrington O. Burrell (1983) expresses some amazement that the House of Lords voted in 1965 to approve the legalization of homosexuality between consenting adults and wonders: 'Could this be one of the reasons for the economic and moral declension in Britain? God gave them up?' To Mr Burrell's way of thinking, since God 'created' sex, he has the right to regulate it. Counsellors should tell victims that homosexuality is 'not just a sickness, but a sin'. The Reverend Barry Chant agrees, noting that the Bible links it with other sins, such as murder, manslaughter, drunkenness, perjury and greed.

It seems to be possible to feel some sympathy for the homosexual man, while remaining rather severe about the homosexual woman. Dr Gilbert Oakley, for instance, applauds the homosexual man's bravery, as evidenced during the last war, but is worried by the proselytizing tendencies of his female counterpart: 'Normal Lesbians usually cease their practices when they reach middle age, but the tribadist persists well past this age. Then, young girls become her objects of passion and desire. Many Lesbians (and vastly out of proportion to male homosexuals) end their days in lunatic asylums.' (Dr Oakley thinks married lesbians can be cured by assuming the 'masculine' role in love-making for a while – 'for so long as it takes her to realize *his* masculine role is the better of the two'.) Dr Chesser thinks the 'genuine homosexual' is suffering from a 'definitely pathological state' but is 'a very likeable person'. Lesbians, on the other hand, 'may constantly seek to seduce normal girls, and win them to their own particular practices . . . A single girl has been known to introduce Lesbianism, which may take various forms, to a whole school . . . There is on record the case of a Polish woman doctor who boasted that she had "seduced more girls and women than anyone else in Poland".'

Or else, members of the jury, you may simply agree with Miss Jane Cousins in describing homosexual sex as being 'as natural as it is for everyone else. What they do and how they give and get sexual pleasure is up to them as individuals.' Dr Comfort thinks all people bisexual. Gays now have their own sex manuals, but Comfort includes bisexuality in *The Joy of Sex*. Gay readers of *More Joy of Sex* are told they may be able to adapt much of the information contained therein: 'The techniques are much the same.'

But most sex manuals that can bring themselves to stray into what Chesser calls 'by-ways of sex' are less concerned with homosexuality than with the sort of activities that they consider to sit on Chesser's thin dividing line between normal and perverse. Or, with what to do when, as 'J' puts it, 'The thing that turns him on you think is sick.' And vice versa, naturally.

Gochros/Fisher's chapter 'When Sex is Distasteful' has a list of the sort of activities they have in mind: 'Any position for intercourse other than that with the male on top, self-stimulation, anal intercourse, oral sex, sex too often, touching your partner's genitals with your hand, making love with the lights on, making love with the lights off, making love anywhere but in bed, making love in or out of the covers, making love with most of your clothes on, making love in the nude, making love'. The authors' 'General Approach to Distasteful Sex' includes many of the same techniques they recommend for tasteful sex. First you draw up a contract and fix a reward and a suitable distress signal ('the distress signal doesn't mean that one of you is chicken or the other one is jerk'). You relax, communicate, and enter into a ten-part programme of negotiation, reaching a formalized agreement at Step 9. Then there is an artlessly titled, nine-step section on 'Making Oral Sex More Tasteful' and a short guide to anal sex ('Other Orifices, Other Appendages'). 'We believe', write Gochros/Fisher, 'that most inhibitions or prohibitions against specific types of sexual activity are undesirable . . . yes, it really seems that our society often robs us of some of the most rewarding, pleasant and satisfying experiences known to human beings, all because of some outmoded ideas about what is right and what is good. It's always useful to ask, "Right for whom? Good for what?" '

The Complete Book of Love and Sex ('Am I odd?') believes that 'foreplay can be the way in which couples, especially younger ones, both express and contain their perverse thoughts and fantasies. This explains why young couples tend to experiment more sexually and this is good because they should in this way slowly evolve a pattern of behaviour which suits them both. In general, a sensible rule is that anything which helps one's partner to greater arousal and better quality orgasms and satisfaction is not only permissible but welcome. So voyeuristic, exhibitionist, oral and even minor sadistic and masochistic acts as well as bondage could well be involved.' All this, they say, is only perverted 'when heterosexual intercourse is consistently by-passed in favour of other sexual activities'. The text is accompanying by a sketch of a young man sitting on an elegant chesterfield about to administer a light spank to the bottom of a smiling girl: 'A Touch of sado-masochism', reads the caption. 'Many couples increase their pleasure by playing games of this type during foreplay.'

But the book warns against 'being locked into non-intercourse sex as your main or only means of sexual release. First, many of the opposite sex will find you strange or unacceptable; second, you will have difficulty finding suitable sex partners; and, last, you could get drawn into all kinds of subcultures in society, many members of which are unusual or unacceptable in other ways.' And how do you recognize a full-blown perversion if you've got one? 'The character-istics are its compulsiveness and its fixity. The person *has* to do it and cannot easily stop doing it.'

'Am I odd?' deals in turn with 'Putting objects in the vagina' (depends what it is – ice cubes OK, small round objects not); sex aids (vibrators OK, penis rings doubtful); anal sex; exhibitionism and voyeurism (OK in private); fetishism (limiting); transvestism and transexualism; and incest (seek help). Second opinions are available elsewhere. Sadism, for instance, comes in for a rough ride from van de Velde: 'in its pronounced form is most hideous, devastating and inhuman [but with its] roots in perfectly normal natures and conditions'. They very name 'masochism', according to Comfort, has outlived its use and 'should be returned to its owner'.

As for fetishes, Chesser talks of 'almost innumerable examples' of them, 'some of them of a most revolting nature . . . Nevertheless, while some fetishes are grossly abnormal, many are harmless enough.' When, says Chesser, they go no further than, say, knickers or shoes and are 'easily met by the love-mate' nobody, he says, is much the worse. There can be problems: 'One woman who sued for divorce mentioned among complaints that her husband insisted on her wearing a cotton petticoat. "I should not have minded so much had he asked me to wear silk underclothes," she told the court.' Distressing for the judge, but there you are. Comfort thinks a fetish becomes a problem only when it overwhelms everything else and becomes a consuming anxiety. People communicating sexually have to 'find their own fidelities'.

As one would expect of such a gourmet, Comfort is unmatched for the sheer variety of practices he outlines, though, naturally, they are all in the main body of the text rather than judgementally sectioned off into autobahns, A roads, B roads, byways or even bridlepaths. *The Joy of Sex* journeys far, wide and alphabetically. So, early on we have *bondage* – 'a venerable human resource'. You won't find it in 'square books'. Try tying each other up while they sleep. 'Ropemarks usually go in a few hours if you've been gentle.' *Boots* – a notorious turn-on – the longer the better. *Chains* – for the tied-up, tinkling look. Uncomfy. *Chastity belt* . . . turns on some people. The fun is in taking it off.

Discipline (beating). 'A kick which either works or it doesn't.' Didn't apparently work for Dr (and Mrs?) Comfort when they tried it. Technique? Start gently at about one blow per second . . . gradually build up force. Canoe and grey birch the best. *Foursomes and moresomes.* Bit of a cult. Alex doesn't himself but sees no reason why others shouldn't – 'plenty do now'. Whether they swop partners is a matter of preference.' *Goldfish* – Two naked people tied and put on mattress together. *Open air* – 'ultimately there will be scheduled areas – we give it another five or six years' (this is 1972). *Party sex* – 'ardent orgiasts' swear by sex parties as one of the main ingredients of a happy marriage. Alex not mad keen himself. But 'I can see the benefit, if you've been married for a long time, of attending an orgy once or twice a year.' *Rubber* – 'A wholesome fetish.' Dry and keep in french chalk. Homely, Alex.

But you have got the general idea by now, and can probably imagine the sections on armpits, stockings, swings, voyeurs, etc. *More Joy of Sex* plays special emphasis on preserving your repertoire on film for posterity, or at the very least for the September years, when one might be forced into less ambitious experiments. Dr Comfort reports that people are using snapshots sexually just as they've previously used them in other family contexts – to jog the memory of good times . . . 'keep an album by all means.' Photographing oneself at it presents its own special difficulties, Dr Comfort concedes: 'Accordingly, photography goes best in a two-couple scene.' One or two further tips: Dr Comfort advises censoring and dividing up any photos before couples go their separate ways – 'and make sure the negatives don't go into the garbage if you mind other folk seeing them.'

There is also advice for those who find themselves unhappily yoked to an armpit junkie or amateur Cartier Bresson. Dr Oakley believes wives have a general duty to understand their husband's little eccentricities. 'What do we mean by understanding? We mean that a wife shall submerge herself into the sexual outlook of her husband, and the husband shall seek to grasp the sexual outlook of his wife.' A subtle difference. But, in Dr Oakley's view, it is 'unwise for a wife to be prim. In the author's casebook-histories are tales of men who, to get full satisfaction with their wives, are compelled to perform sexual acts wearing girl's underwear. Sometimes, even skirts or dresses. Some other cases show that men, to get ultimate satisfaction, must perform the act so they can see their movements and those of their wives in a mirror . . . Such acts are distasteful to many wives and cause the most dreadful rows and ultimate separation on the grounds of mental cruelty and so forth.' And Dr Oakley's view? 'The mental cruelty originates in the minds of the "wives" who are not sophisticated enough to realize that, in the husband's sexual background, lurks some event that gives rise to the present desire to resurrect past joys with present pleasure – *and* with the women of his final choice.'

'J' thinks it all a matter of degree. For instance, 'an astonishing number of men find black garter belts, high heels and sheer black stockings highly erotic. I personally think they look garish, but if the man I love wanted me to wear that get-up I would from time to time, and so should you . . . if you are given completely wicked nightwear, blush if you must, but wear it with pride and often . . . unless you have an ultra-strong aversion to his pet sexual practice, be a good sport and make it pleasurable for him.' On the other hand, he may have his sights on some of Dr Comfort's more enterprising assignments. 'J' is less sympathetic if so: 'If he wants to resort to whips and chains or have you urinate on him or something of that nature, I agree with you, I think he's sick – and he should let you alone and go find a simpatico sickie, or, better yet, get professional help.'

One way to convince your partner that what you want to do is not so sick may be to take him/her to a sample swapping/sharing evening, as described in *More Joy of Sex*: 'You can learn more in one session by watching a few other couples than out of this whole book,' says Dr Comfort unassumingly.

Enough!

I am so sorry, m'lud.

The case is adjourned.

14

French and Other Methods

Doctors will doubtless blame their learned friends in the law. Look, they will say accusingly, at the unhappy case of Annie Besant and Charles Bradlaugh, prosecuted in 1877 by the Solicitor General himself for printing and distributing contraceptive advice. Look at the associated case of Edward Truelove, a bookseller in his late sixties, sent to jail for four months for selling Knowlton's *The Fruits of Philosophy*, a text already forty-five years out of date. Is it any wonder, doctors will say, that their forebears were, well, cautious about making great shows of enlightenment concerning the advent of birth control?

M'learned friends will doubtless reply that the excuse is a pretty watery one. They will point to the case, eight years later, of Dr H. A. Allbutt from Leeds – struck off the Medical Register for publishing and selling *The Wife's Handbook*, which described the condom, douche, sponge and diaphragm as well as casting doubt on the reliability of the safe period. His own medical colleagues deplored the dissemination of advice available 'at so low a price as to bring the work within the reach of the youth of both sexes, to the detriment of public morals'. He was, judged the General Medical Council, guilty of 'infamous conduct in a professional respect'. Why blame the lawyers?

Whose-ever the blame, the action against Messrs Besant, Bradlaugh, Truelove and Allbutt seems to have been enough to have dissuaded most doctors from similarly openly risking their careers. Even learned dissertations shrank from discussion. G. H. Darwin, a fellow of the Royal College of Physicians, can be found in 1884 talking simply of 'certain practices, much more common in America, and on the continent of Europe, but not altogether unknown amongst ourselves, by which it is sought to limit the number of children brought into a family, or to entirely prevent conception'. Such practices, he asserts, cause uterine disease – 'especially those of chemical or mechanical means, which [work] in a clumsy and coarse fashion'. And with that he declines to venture any further into 'repulsive detail' (paper on *Leuchorrhoea or The Whites*).

In the light of such establishment revulsion it is not wholly surprising that Dr Allbutt's *Wife's Handbook* should subsequently have achieved enormous sales. But the medical/ethical debate over contraception that romped on for twenty, thirty, forty more years retreated for a while into the safer pages of the professional journals. It is worth remembering, though, that as late as 1917 the report of the National Birth Rate Commission contains the testimony of most eminent doctors asserting that prolonged use of contraceptives reduces fertility, causes physical, mental and moral harm and is, in short, 'race suicide'.

Even this is tame stuff set beside the opinions of Lyman B. Sperry in 1900. He tackles the ethical issues head-on, writing of 'artificial' methods that 'in many cases . . . are abominable, not simply because they are unhealthy but because they are so much employed by those monsters in human form who are encouraged by them to the perpetration of seduction and adultery. They serve to cultivate the damnable conduct that breaks the hearts of so many parents and leads to the destruction of so many homes.' Eugenic reasons are the only plausible ones for attempting even the 'sterile period' method of conception control – those couples 'who feel they *must* occasionally indulge in copulation, and yet know they ought to prevent conception'. They know who they are – those who are 'physically, mentally and morally unfit to bring children into the world'.

Sperry is a touch vague as to the fine details of the sterile period, which he thinks runs 'as a rule from about the 12th or 14th day after the cessation of each menstrual flow to a day or so preceding the next menstruation'. Those ten or twelve days, he considers, 'furnish all the opportunity that any reasonable couple can demand from sexual indulgence. A man who cannot, or will not, accommodate himself to such conditions when necessary, is so brutal a sex glutton that no woman ought to be required to live with him.'

But does the method work? Well, since you mention it, not terribly well. Sperry admits that it is ineffective for between a quarter and a tenth of British and American women: 'Indeed, there are a few who are almost sure to conceive whenever semen is allowed to enter the vagina – provided, of course, they are not already pregnant.' Of course. 'The only way of each woman to determine this matter is by trial, but, while experimenting, she may repeatedly become pregnant, and finally learn that at no time during any month is she exempt from the possibilities of pregnancy.'

Not an encouraging prognosis. But Sperry's problem is that he believes all other artificial methods of contraception to be unreliable at best, positively harmful at worst. 'The protracted interruption or total suspension of any natural physiological activity is sure to prove to some extent pernicious, if not indeed seriously destructive . . . hence for any couple to live in the marriage relation, indulging frequently in sexual congress and yet preventing conception must be, in some measure, injurious to both of them.'

As so often, it is the Continentals who are to blame. There is no doubt in Sperry's mind that 'French methods' are the greatest liability, both to health and peace of mind. Those readers who are not Francophiles are advised that the methods of that country 'consist of a thin sack, called a "safe" or "cundum" ' which is liable to break at any moment. 'Safes that can be confidently depended on have never yet been made and no-one who uses them can feel comfortably confident at any time.'

'But these French devices', he adds, 'are not only untrustworthy; they are unsatisfactory and injurious, both to the males and to the females who use them. They are nearly, if not quite, as dangerous to the health as masturbation and Onanism. The semen of the male especially when mingled with the natural secretions of the female vagina, is nature's healthful balm for the tissues that become so congested during copulation.' Vaginas denied this soothing unction are subject to 'unnatural and irritating engorgement' which, if allowed to persist, leads to 'enslaving sexual desire which, while demanding frequent gratification, is seldom satisfied. Through the habitual use of safes, *satyriasts* may soon become chronic in the males and *nymphomanis* may be established in the females. It is impossible to determine definitively which is the most harmful, masturbation, Onanism or the use of "French safe".'

'Onanism' is used in its proper context of *coitus interruptus* – 'an abomination', according to Sperry: 'Decidedly unreliable . . . seriously detrimental to health. For males, the practice is nearly as

disastrous as masturbation . . . a cause of weakness and disease.'
Caps, a.k.a. womb veils and rubber dams are little better – 'the
anatomical structure of many females is such that these veils
cannot be made effective.' Douches are, says Sperry, even less
reliable than Onanism. Carbolic acid, borax, sulphates of zinc,
vinegar, salt, ammonia and patent pills are all to be avoided. Cold
water is 'a positive danger': patent suppositories are 'Satanic
devices'. Nor do they work.

This leaves only total abstinence, which Sperry thinks 'practically impossible' in most cases, or the complete avoidance of the
male climax, a.k.a. Zugassent's Discovery or Karezza. So interested in this method was Sperry that he delayed publication of the
book for a year the better to investigate it. The method did not
emerge unscathed from this investigation. All the couples he asked
to try it failed to make it work properly, experiencing instead
'nerve tension and spinal congestion . . . frequently followed by
lascivious dreams and seminal emissions during the disturbed
sleep that succeeds the indulgence'. Karezza, Sperry concludes, is
a 'delusion and a snare', useful only for 'cold-blooded, semi-sexed
men and passionless women, or old and sexually decaying men and
women [and] certain grades of exhausted libertines whose dwarfed
testicles and leaden nerves tell of incipient impotency'.

It is no great surprise, after this, to come across Marie Stopes
bemoaning the general ignorance on contraception eighteen years
later. She speaks in *Wise Parenthood* of a woman doctor who knew of
no contraceptive method after fifteen years in the job. Marie
Stopes, while light years ahead of Dr Sperry in her views on birth
control, seems to share his distaste for those who fail to live up to
proper eugenic standards. She has a patriotic view of contraception
– 'to bring forth children for the Empire who have the best chance
which that pair can give them of health and beauty and happiness'.
She talks of unfit weaklings and diseased children and observes:
'The work of the Empire is hindered and its existence jeopardized
if our people are so hampered. The majestic destiny of the human
race can only be fulfilled when all are strong, beautiful and
intelligent. Hence only children with the chance of attaining such a
maturity should be conceived.'

The moral debate about contraception rather peters out in sex
manuals after Marie Stopes and the Great War, which finally saw
British troops being officially issued with condoms – to protect

them against VD more than the potential of parenthood. But this does not stop one or two Christian writers from attempting to resuscitate it from time to time. A plucky rearguard action is put up by Geldenhuys in 1952, in which he sets out four false motives for using birth control: the love of wealth, luxury and ease; shirking the uncomfortable inconvenience of pregnancy and birth; the idea that small families are beneficial to parents, children or the community ('the larger the family, the less likely divorce'); and the fear of overpopulating the world ('With the scientific development of agriculture there is little likelihood that with proper distribution a considerably increased population could not be fed.') He adds, echoing across the generations: 'It must also be said here that contraception, in practice, *often leads to sexual dissipation* and this is not only outside of marriage where it allows for sexual intercourse between people who are not entitled to it, but also inside marriage, where the use of contraceptives often results in too frequent sexual intercourse and may lead to nervous disorders.' More daringly still, Geldenhuys proceeds to an awesome warning about the physical effects of birth control. He speaks of couples who decide to delay having children who feel 'piteous dismay on discovering that sterility has set in with one or both of them as a result of the constant use of artificial contraceptives, or of too frequent sexual intercourse.' His own feeling is that 'a reasonable number of children is indispensable to the fullest joy of home life, and it is gross stupidity wilfully to confine the number to one or two . . . And the parents who wisely rear a good-sized family with joy and faith are the blessed of the earth.'

The ethical debate eventually gives way to discussion about the virtues of various methods, beginning with *sheaths*. Marie Stopes, considering varieties of rubber, skin and treated silk condoms, is doubtful about their value since they prevent semen enriching the woman, though she concedes that they are a good way of preventing the semen of ill men reaching women. Chesser talks of recent improvement in quality, though advises: 'always inflate the condom . . . hold it up against a strong light. This may reveal a pinhole. I was once told by a girl who had been employed in a rubber goods factory that some of the employees made pinpricks in the finished products. It was their idea of a joke.' Ryley Scott is just as suspicious: 'Blow into the tube until it swells out like a toy balloon and then, holding it by the top, squeeze very gently, at the same passing it over the face, and note if there is any escape of air.' He advises keeping them in a dark place: 'They should not be carried around for indefinite periods in one's waistcoat pocket.'

Stopes considers that *caps* should be used in combination with a soluble quinine pessary (based on cocoa butter), though she wonders whether quinine might be absorbed into the woman, leading to sleeplessness or digestive interference. Geldenhuys warns against all 'rubber mechanisms' in the vagina on grounds of hygiene. He cites cases where contraceptive cream has harmed sperm, thereby producing deformed children. Caps can also, he says, cause cancer. Furthermore, they are awkward, notes Chesser, for women with short fingers. He recommends glycero-gelatin, cocoa-butter and soap suppositories and gels – easy and 'moreover they are easily concealed – a point which will appeal to those who have suffered embarrassment when passing through customs with contraceptive apparatus in their trunks'.

Straightforward *douching* is rather frowned on by Stopes. She thinks it rather an indignity for the wife to jump out of bed just when she wants to sleep, and with her husband already nodded off. 'She also suffers from the local chill of getting up out of a warm bed and moving about the room, unless she is one of the very few fortunate ones who can afford a fire in the bedroom and a maid to prepare the warm douche.' If a maid is available, use vinegar or common salt and water. Chesser thinks it inadvisable by itself, but of value when used with other methods – suggests boric acid, lysol, vinegar, potassium permanganate or else a small teaspoon of salt to a pint of water.

Stopes is even more severe on the rhythm method, claiming that male sperm can live for eight to ten days. Weatherhead is more favourable. 'Twice or once a month is often found to be sufficient for the self-controlled man, though unfortunately this so-called "safe period" coincides with a woman's disinclination and not her desire.' Lucia Radl commends it as 'well-established . . . universally accepted by the medical profession and church authorities' while Geldenhuys gives pages of diagrams, charts and algebraic calculations (m-$1p$ $[18-11] = 17$ etc.). He says it is 97 per cent reliable, quoting one source who found 'not one pregnancy reported by any couple who followed the system faithfully'. Most books attacking the method (van de Velde, for instance) were, he says, written before the recent discoveries of Dr Kyusaka Ogino

(1929) and Hermann Knaus. *The Complete Book of Love and Sex* (1983) quotes Family Planning Association figures showing the method to be between 85 and 93 per cent safe. Alex Comfort calls it vatican roulette.

Coitus interruptus gets an unmixed and derogatory press. Van de Velde calls it 'conjugal fraud', with 'infinitely serious' physical effects for the wife. 'Not only a degradation, but also an extermination of the marital relationship.' Weatherhead thinks it likely to cause neurosis and nervous breakdown. 'The practice cannot be too strongly condemned.' Geldenhuys considers the method causes husbands 'excessive expenditure of nervous energy . . . concentrating on the exact moment of interruption causes great nervous strain, upsetting the mental and spiritual balance as well. Such men become irritable, and may become subject to sudden violent bursts of temper. In extreme cases they may develop most unpleasant physical and nervous symptoms.' May cause similar symptoms and 'crying fits' in women.

Other miscellaneous and emergency methods crop up. Stopes recommends a sponge soaked in soap powder or a cotton wool pad smeared with vaseline mixed with powdered borax. Chesser describes how to use rubber sponges, cotton wool or animal wool coated in common alum, household vinegar and lemon juice or fats and oils. Ryley Scott suggests a handkerchief rolled into a ball and dipped in olive oil or soapy water as the best makeshift arrangement.

The Pill makes its first triumphant entrance in the mid-60s, shortly after the more reliable forms of the IUD. 'The best kind of contraceptive available today,' trumpets Wardell B. Pomeroy in 1969. 'Its use has even inspired a Hollywood film.' Eleanor Hamilton briefly notes some reports of blood clots in the same year, but thinks that other side effects 'generally disappear fairly rapidly'. Within ten years Jane Cousins is warning the over-thirties off it and calling for more research into its dangers. Another six years and Sheila Kitzinger is dwelling at length on the side effects and pronouncing: 'It is not the solution to contraceptive worries for many women. In coping with fertility fairly effectively, it poses fresh problems and introduces new anxieties.'

Anne Hooper in 1983 pronounces herself 'not thrilled' with the choice of birth control methods available, but exhorts women to take heart. 'By the end of the 1980s', she predicts, 'there could be dozens of alternatives to choose from.' Hormones, Coilatex sponges, Jost intravaginal devices, Contracaps, spermicide-releasing rings, contraceptive gels which swell in the vagina, nasal sprays and pregnancy vaccination. She further predicts that the Billings method of determining the safe period will lead to a fashion for women wearing basal body thermometers around the neck as pendants. The Billingses being Australian, not French, even Lyman B. Sperry himself might have approved. But there again, probably not.

15

A Peculiar Thrill or Glow

So much for you adults. But what to tell the children? A promising start is to keep a pet. Charles Thompson, as editor of *Health and Efficiency*, should be heeded: 'The phenomenon of the increase in the family of the rabbit; the mystery of the newly-hatched pigeons, and so on, present the opportunity for wise explanation. The whole matter can be invested with a halo of glory and of reverence, and it is an easy transition to the realm of the human' (1917). All in good time. Walter Gallichan (1919) puts in a word for a study of butterflies and pond life in addition to keeping pets. 'Many important introductory lessons in sex education may be learned in the woods, and on the moors and hills.'

A sample morning might run something like this. Begin: 'This morning let us walk across the meadow to the copse and look for a bird's nest. I want to show you a blackbird's home with the eggs in it.' When you reach the nest try something on these lines: 'You have asked me how you came to life and I will tell you. You have learned already several interesting and wonderful things about the coming to life of some insects, birds, fishes and cats. When your father and I knew that we loved one another, and were married, I hoped that I might have a baby of my very own, and so did your father. One day I felt a little live creature was beginning to grow in me . . . At last you had grown big enough to come into the world and to leave the warm nest. Like the chickens in the eggs, you wanted to come out and you found the way.'

You need not use these exact words, of course. You might prefer those of Emma Drake (1901) upon reaching her nest and pointing to the little bird atop its little egg: 'In much the same way, my darling, you grew; only instead of your being able to see the little egg, it was kept warm and snug in a little room in mamma's body, while you grew from a tiny speck of an egg . . . into a fat, beautiful rollicking baby . . . you came out through a little door made purposely for it.'

G. Stanley Hall (1911) reports that 'some think, at least for girls, all that is needed can be taught by means of flowers and their fertilization, and that mature years will bring insight enough to apply it all to human life. Others would demonstrate on the cadaver so that in the presence of death knowledge may be given without passions. This I once saw in Paris, but cannot commend it for general use.' But you may find that using animal or plant life helps you, as well as your child. The Reverend the Hon. E. Lyttelton (1900) is emphatic that the 'national characteristic' of shyness 'has always been the grand obstacle to the giving of salutary instruction of this sort to the young ... If a father, desirous of beginning with the easier part of the subject, adopts the botanical illustration in order to lead up to a personal appeal, he will find that his difficulty, when he comes to the point, has been very slightly diminished by the scientific preamble.'

Who should do the telling? Lyttelton thinks that 'there seems to be a natural division of labour between the two parents. Suppose the mother takes upon herself to lay the foundations of the knowledge at about eight or nine years of age: there remains a necessary caution to be given to boys towards the time of puberty, which, properly speaking, ought to be somewhat medical in character, and this would seem to be the part either of the father or of some trustworthy doctor.' Thompson believes that fathers should tell their sons the basics: 'He is a thrice-blessed father who can take his boy out for a walk in the country and find in the hedgerows, or in the sweet picture of the sheep and the lamb, object lessons of life.' Weatherhead thinks Mother is best.

Try some sample conversations. Here is one recommended by Marie Stopes:

'Daddy and Mummy enjoyed making you much more than you enjoy playing with bricks.'

'Where was I kept?'

'What is the warmest, softest, safest place you can think of? Mummy's heart; that is all warm with love. The place Mummy hid you while God and she were making you was right underneath her heart.'

Or this, from Mary Ware Dennet (1918): 'When a man and a woman fall in love so that they really belong to each other, the physical side of the relation is this; both of them feel at intervals a peculiar thrill or glow, particularly in the sexual organs, and it naturally culminates after they have gone to bed at night.' Or this, from Frances Strain (1936): 'Outwardly, the father and mother lie close together, arms about each other, while the sperm-bearing fluid enters into the mother by way of perfectly-fitting passages.'

Lyttelton thinks the right time to strike with boys is just as they go off to school. 'The parent can perfectly well add that the seed of life is entrusted by God to the father in a very wonderful way, and that after marriage he is allowed to give it to his wife, this being on his part an act of the love which first made him marry her. Seldom, I should fancy, would more than that he required in the case of girl children. The only difference in the case of boys would be that, quite simply and delicately, use should be made of the innate instinct as to indicate with distinctness what portion of his body will have the propagation of life entrusted to it as its natural function; and, based on this instruction, an impressive warning may be given against misuse.

'I am inclined to think that this could be done in very simple language, without any reference being made to plants. The warning should be against meddling with something precious and sacred . . . Some, however, might find it useful to explain about the fertilization of plants in order to picture the mischief to either male or female if the organs were rudely opened when the plant was still young. It would not die, but would be robbed of its most wonderful endowment.'

Gallichan is less certain about the wisdom of drawing attention to these parts: 'The less thought given to the sexual organs during the time of growth in childhood and youth the better . . . thought should not be idly directed, or without real necessity, upon organs which have not fully developed and are not yet ready for the great and solemn racial use.'

The Complete Book of Love and Sex (1983) sample conversation runs as follows:

'Where do babies come from?'

'They grow in Mummy's tummy after Daddy puts a seed there.'

'Where does Daddy get the seeds from?'

'They grow inside his body in the things that hang down behind his penis.'

'How do they get into Mummy's tummy?'

'Daddy and Mummy cuddle up together and he puts his penis into her vagina and seeds come out inside her.'

'Can I watch it?'

'Well, we'd rather you didn't because we like to be alone when we're doing it.'

Don't forget the moral principles. Tim and Beverly LaHaye (1976) believe that 'teaching sex without moral principles is like pouring gasoline on a fire . . . the last thing the adolescent male needs is exposure to sexually igniting information that will not be used for several years.' Indeed, Tim and Beverly recommend delaying the acquisition of in-depth knowledge about sex until just before your children's wedding. 'A few good books on the subject studied carefully two or three weeks before marriage, a frank discussion with their family doctor and pastoral counselling usually are adequate preparation.'

It is difficult to improve upon Gallichan's instructions on moral principles. He urges teachers and parents to impress upon the young that the struggle for chastity 'may be likened to an athletic contest . . . it should be insisted that strength of will is manly, that virility endures if it has not been abused.' Sexual appetites must be disciplined: 'If this impulse is not properly controlled', parents should tell their young, 'it may cause the deepest misery to ourselves and to those whom we love.'

'Every great philanthropist is an instance of the sublimation of the sexual instinct' (parents should continue). 'The virile man uses his virility in many ways besides reproduction. St Francis, who possessed this vital power in abundance, refrained from all conduct likely to impair him and devoted his love force to deeds of kindness among the poor . . . Byron was a man of remarkable vital forces which he frequently failed to sublimate. There are episodes of failure in the life of this impulsive genius. On the other hand, there was effort towards sublimation of the racial energy, as was shown by Byron's devotion to the cause of oppressed humanity, his tendance upon the sick and wounded, and his enthusiasm for art . . . Remember that one foolish or evil action that threatens chastity may poison the whole of a man's future life. One hour of folly has often proved disastrous.' Gallichan is keen to impress upon youth how far mankind has succeeded in elevating himself above the basely passions of animals. 'It has', he says, 'needed millions of years to develop the instinct of lowly animals for mating into the exalted love of a Browning or a Kingsley.' He was, of course, denied the benefit of the more recent scholastic insights into Kingsley's personal life.

There is, needless to say, a specialist literature for the younger reader, not considered here – a microcosm of the grown-up canon. Sometimes writers of adult books produce scaled-down works for aspiring adults. The Reverend Dr Sylvanus Stall, author of *What a Young Man Ought to Know*, wrote also *What a Young Boy Ought to Know* for the under-sixteen market and *Almost a Man* for the lucrative teenage sector. Helena Wright followed up *The Sex Factor in Marriage* in 1930 with *What is Sex?* two years later (revamped as *Sex, an Outline for Young People* in 1963). Parents today contemplating embarking on one of the more elaborate sex-improvement course will be pleased to come across a lilliputian version in Joani Blank's *Playbook for Kids About Sex* (1982). The sexpieces and questionnaires of, say, Brown/Faulder or Nowinski are mirrored in the forty or so pages of drawings, exercises and multiple-choice sections for the pre-pubescent reader. What is sexy? What is a sexy person? Write all the different words you've heard for boy's/men's/girl's/women's parts. ('It's okay to write words you've heard that are not nice.') Draw your penis/female sex parts. Did you ever have an orgasm? Once or twice/all the time/not sure/not yet/don't care? There is a five-page section on masturbation ('Touching yourself to feel good'). How do you do it? Like anyone in the following nine illustrations? Then three pages on intercourse followed by four on sexual orientation.

The final two paces are left blank for reader participation. One is titled: 'On this page you can write some daydreams about a person or some people you might want to have sex with when you grow up.' The other reads: 'If you think this book is just really gross you can write about it here.'

Thus we close, appropriately handing on the torch to another generation. And with that you could, if you've found *this* book just really gross, write about it here . . .

Bibliography

Baden-Powell, Lord, *Rovering to Success*, Herbert Jenkins Ltd, London, 1930.

Barbach, Lonnie Garfield, PhD, *For Yourself; The Fulfillment of Female Sexuality*, Signet, New York, 1975.

Blackwell, Dr Elizabeth, *The Human Element in Sex*, J&A Churchill, Edinburgh and London, 1884.

Blank, Joani, *The Playbook for Kids About Sex*, Sheba, London, 1982.

Board of Education, *Sex Education in Schools and Youth Organizations*, HMSO, London, 1943.

Brecher, Edward M., *The Sex Researchers*, Deutsch, London, 1969.

Brown, Gabrielle, PhD, *The New Celibacy: How to Take a Vacation from Sex and Enjoy it*, Ballantine Books, New York, 1980.

Brown, Helen Gurley, *Having It All*, Sidgwick and Jackson, London, 1982.

Brown, Paul and Faulder, Carolyn, *Treat Yourself to Sex: A Guide for Good Loving*, Dent, London, 1977.

Burrell, Barrington O., *Love, Sex and Marriage*, 1983 (no publishers listed).

Carpenter, Edward, *Marriage in a Free Society*, The Labour Press Society Ltd, Manchester, 1894.

Cauthery, Philip and Stanway, Drs Andrew and Penny, *The Complete Book of Love and Sex: A Guide for All the Family*, Century Publishing, London, 1983.

Chance, Janet, *The Cost of English Morals*, Noel Douglas, London, 1931.

Chant, Barry, *Straight Talk About Sex*, Whittaker, USA, 1977.

Chesser, Dr Eustace, *Love Without Fear: A Plain Guide to Sex Technique for Every Married Adult*, Rich and Cowan, London, 1941.

Chesser, Dr Eustace, *Woman and Love*, Jarrolds, London, 1962.

Comfort, Alex, *The Anxiety Makers: Some Curious Preoccupations of the Medical Profession*, Nelson, London, 1967.

Comfort, Alex, *The Joy of Sex*, Quartet, London, 1972.

Comfort, Alex, *More Joy of Sex*, Mitchell Beazley, London, 1975.

Cornerstone of Reconstruction: A Book on Working for Social Purity Among Men, By Four Chaplains to the Forces, SPCK, London, 1919.

Cousins, Jane, *Make it Happy: What Sex is All About*, Virago, London, 1978.

Darwin, G. H., *Leuchorroea, or the Whites*, John Heywood, London, 1884.

Dennet, Mary Ware, *The Sex Side of Life: An Explanation for Young People*, 1918.

Drake, Emma Angell, MD, *What a Young Wife Ought to Know*, Self and Sex Series, Philadelphia, 1901.

Ellis, Havelock, *On Life and Sex*, A. & C. Black Ltd, London, 1920.

Ethelmer, Ellis, *Phases of Love: As it Was; As it Is; As it May Be*, privately published, Congleton, 1897.

Exner, Dr M. J., *The Sexual Side of Marriage*, George Allen and Unwin, London, 1932.

Eyles, Leonora, *Sex for the Engaged*, Hale, London, 1952.

Gallichan, Walter, *A Textbook of Sex Education For Parents and Teachers*, T. Werner Laurie, London, 1919.

Geldenhuys, Norval, *The Intimate Life: Or, The Christian's Sex Life, A practical, up-to-date handbook intended for engaged and newly-married Christians*, James Clarke, London, 1952.

Gochros, Harvey and Fisher, Joel, *Treat Yourself to a Better Sex Life*, Prentice-Hall, New Jersey, 1980.

Griffith, Edward, MRCS, *Sex and Citizenship*, Gollancz, London, 1941.

Guyot, Jules, *Breviare del'Amour experimental*, 1859; republished Noel Douglas, London, 1931.

Hall, G. Stanley, *Adolescence*, D. Appleton, New York and London, 1911.

Havil, Anthony, *Toward a Better Understanding of Sexual Relationship*, Wales Publishing Co., London, 1939.

Heath, Stephen, *The Sexual Fix*, Macmillan, London, 1982.

Heiman, Julia and Lopiccolo, Leslie and Joseph, *Becoming Orgasmic: A Sexual Growth Program for Women*, Prentice-Hall, New Jersey, 1976.

Hirschfeld, Magnus, *Sexual Anomalies and Perversions*, Torch Publishing Co., London, n.d.

Hutton, Isabel Emslie, CBE, MD, *The Hygiene of Marriage*, Heinemann, London, 1953.

'J', *The Sensuous Woman: The First How-to Book for the Female Who Yearns to be All Woman*, W. H. Allen and Lyle Stuart Inc., London and New York, 1970.

Kitzinger, Sheila, *Woman's Experience of Sex*, Dorling Kindersley, London, 1983.

Landau, Rom, *Sex, Life and Faith*, Faber, London, 1946.

LaHaye, Tim and Beverly, *The Act of Marriage*, Zondervan, Michigan, 1976.

Longshore-Potts, Mrs A. M., MD, *Love, Courtship and Marriage*, published by author, London and San Diego, 1895.

Lyttelton, Rev. the Hon. E., *Training of the Young in Laws of Sex*, Longmans, London, 1900.

MacAndrew, Rennie, *Life Long Love: Healthy Sex and Marriage*, Wales Publishing Co., London, 1928.

Morgan, Marabel, *The Total Woman*, Fleming H. Revell, USA, 1973; Hodder & Stoughton, London, 1975.

Nowinski, Joseph, *Becoming Satisfied: A Man's Guide to Self-fulfilment*, Prentice-Hall, New Jersey, 1976.

Oakley, Gilbert, *Sane and Sensual Sex*, Walton Press, London, 1963.

Parkinson-Smith, E., *The Physical Content of Marriage*, Wales Publishing Co., London, 1952.

Penland, L. R., 'Sex Education in 1900, 1940 and 1980', *Journal of School Health*, 51.305–9.

Penney, Alexandra, *How To Make Love to a Man*, Clarkson Potter Inc., New York, 1981.

'A Physician', *For Men Only*, Cecil Palmer, London, 1925.

Pomeroy, Wardell B., *Girls and Sex*, Delacorte Press, 1969.

Preparation for Marriage, A handbook prepared by a special committee on behalf of the British Social Hygiene Council, Cape, London, 1932.

Radl, Lucia, MD, *Illustrated Guide to Sex Happiness in Marriage*, Heinemann, London, 1953.

Rainer, Jerome and Julia, *Sexual Adventure in Marriage*, Anthony Blond, London, 1966.

Reid, Gavin, *Starting Out Together: A Book for Those Contemplating Marriage*, Hodder and Stoughton, London, 1981.

Sadler, William S., *Courtship and Love*, Macmillan, New York, 1952.

Sandford, Dr Christine, *Enjoy Sex in the Middle Years*, Martin Dunitz, London, 1983.

SAR (Sexual Attitude Restructuring): Guide for a Better Sex Life, National Sex Forum, San Francisco, 1975.

Scott, George Ryley, *Your Sex Questions Answered*, Knole Park Press, Sevenoaks, 1947.

Smedes, Lewis, *Sex in the Real World*, Eeerdmans, Grand Rapids, USA, 1976.

Sperry, Lyman B., AM, MD, *Confidential Talks with Husband and Wife: A Book of Information and Advice for the Married and Marriageable*, Oliphant Anderson and Ferrier, Edinburgh and London, 1900.

Stopes, Marie, *Wise Parenthood: A Book for Married People*, A. C. Fifield, London, 1918.

Stopes, Marie, *Radiant Motherhood*, G. P. Putnam, London, 1920.

Stopes, Marie, *Married Love: A New Contribution to Sex Difficulties*, G. P. Putnam, London, 1923.

Strain, Frances B., *Being Born*, Meredith Corp., Des Moines, 1936.

Trobisch, Walter, *I Loved a Girl*, Lutterworth Press, Guildford, 1963.

Van de Velde, *Ideal Marriage: Its Physiology and Technique*, Heinemann, London, 1930.

Wright, Helena, MB, BS, *Sex, an Outline for Young People*, Ernest Benn, London, 1963.

Wright, Helena, *The Sex Factor in Marriage*, Noel Douglas, London, 1930.

Weatherhead, Leslie D., *The Mastery of Sex Through Psychology and Religion*, SCMP, London, 1931.